The Short Story Series

GENERAL EDITOR JAMES GIBSON

ADVENTURE
AMERICAN
ANIMAL
COUNTRY
CRIME
DETECTION
FANTASY
HORROR
HUMOUR
LOVE
SCIENCE FICTION
SEA
SPORT
SUPERNATURAL
SUSPENSE
TRAVEL
WAR
WESTERN

fantasy, phantasy, *n.* fancy: imagination: mental image: love (*obs.*): caprice: fantasia: a story . . . not based on realistic characters or setting: preoccupation with thoughts associated with unobtainable desires.

Chambers Twentieth Century Dictionary

Fantasy

CHOSEN BY
Alyn Shipton

John Murray
Albemarle Street London

Typeset by Inforum Ltd, Portsmouth.
Printed and bound in Great Britain
by Butler and Tanner Ltd,
Frome and London

British Library Cataloguing in Publication Data

Fantasy. – (The Short story series)
1. Children's stories, English
I. Shipton, Alyn
823′ .01′089282 [J]   PZ5

ISBN 0-7195-3874-2

Contents

The Cat-hood of Maurice

To have your hair cut is not painful, nor does it hurt to have your whiskers trimmed. But round wooden shoes, shaped like bowls, are not comfortable wear, however much it may amuse the on-looker to see you try to walk in them. If you have a nice fur coat like a company promoter's, it is most annoying to be made to swim in it. And if you had a tail, surely it would be solely your own affair; that any one should tie a tin can to it would strike you as an unwarrantable impertinence—to say the least.

Yet it is difficult for an outsider to see these things from the point of view of both the persons concerned. To Maurice, scissors in hand, alive and earnest to snip, it seemed the most natural thing in the world to shorten the stiff whiskers of Lord Hugh Cecil by a generous inch. He did not understand how useful those whiskers were to Lord Hugh, both in sport and in the more serious business of getting a living. Also it amused Maurice to throw Lord Hugh into ponds, though Lord Hugh only once permitted this liberty. To put walnuts on Lord Hugh's feet and then to watch him walk on ice was, in Maurice's opinion, as good as a play. Lord Hugh was a very favourite cat, but Maurice was discreet, and Lord Hugh, except under violent suffering, was at that time anyhow, dumb.

But the empty sardine-tin attached to Lord Hugh's tail and hind legs—this had a voice, and, rattling against stairs, banisters, and the legs of stricken furniture, it cried aloud for vengeance. Lord Hugh, suffering violently, added his voice, and this time the family heard. There was a chase, a chorus of 'Poor pussy!' and 'Pussy, then!' and the tail and the tin and Lord Hugh were caught under Jane's bed. The tail and the tin acquiesced in their rescue. Lord Hugh did not. He fought, scratched, and bit. Jane carried the scars of that rescue for many a long week.

When all was calm Maurice was sought and, after some little natural delay, found—in the boot-cupboard.

'Oh, Maurice!' his mother almost sobbed, 'how *can* you? What will your father say?'

Maurice thought he knew what his father would do.

'Don't you know,' the mother went on, 'how wrong it is to be cruel?'

'I didn't mean to be cruel,' Maurice said. And, what is more, he spoke the truth. All the unwelcome attentions he had showered on Lord Hugh had not been exactly intended to hurt that stout veteran—only it was interesting to see what a cat would do if you threw it in the water, or cut its whiskers, or tied things to its tail.

'Oh, but you must have meant to be cruel,' said mother, 'and you will have to be punished.'

'I wish I hadn't,' said Maurice, from the heart.

'So do I,' said his mother, with a sigh; 'but it isn't the first time; you know you tied Lord Hugh up in a bag with the hedgehog only last Tuesday week. You'd better go to your room and think it over. I shall have to tell your father directly he comes home.'

Maurice went to his room and thought it over. And the more he thought the more he hated Lord Hugh. Why couldn't the beastly cat have held his tongue and sat still? That, at the time would have been a disappointment, but now Maurice wished it had happened. He sat on the edge of his bed and savagely kicked the edge of the green Kidderminster carpet, and hated the cat.

He hadn't meant to be cruel; he was sure he hadn't; he wouldn't have pinched the cat's feet or squeezed its tail in the door, or pulled its whiskers, or poured hot water on it. He felt himself ill-used, and knew that he would feel still more so after the inevitable interview with his father.

But that interview did not take the immediately painful form expected by Maurice. His father did *not* say, 'Now I will show you what it feels like to be hurt.' Maurice had braced himself for that, and was looking beyond it to the calm of forgiveness which should follow the storm in which he should so unwillingly take part. No; his father was already calm and reasonable—with a dreadful calm, a terrifying reason.

'Look here, my boy,' he said. 'This cruelty to dumb animals must be checked—severely checked.'

'I didn't mean to be cruel,' said Maurice.

'Evil,' said Mr Basingstoke, for such was Maurice's surname, 'is wrought by want of thought as well as want of heart. What about your putting the hen in the oven?'

'You know,' said Maurice, pale but determined, 'you *know* I only wanted to help her to get her eggs hatched quickly. It says in "Fowls for Food and Fancy" that heat hatches eggs.'

'But she hadn't any eggs,' said Mr Basingstoke.

'But she soon would have,' urged Maurice. 'I thought a stitch in time—'

'That,' said his father, 'is the sort of thing that you must learn not to think.'

'I'll try,' said Maurice, miserably hoping for the best.

'I intend that you shall,' said Mr Basingstoke. 'This afternoon you go to Dr Strongitharm's for the remaining week of term. If I find any more cruelty taking place during the holidays you will go there permanently. You can go and get ready.'

'Oh, father, *please* not,' was all Maurice found to say.

'I'm sorry, my boy,' said his father, much more kindly; 'it's all for your own good, and it's as painful to me as it is to you— remember that. The cab will be here at four. Go and put your things together, and Jane shall pack for you.'

So the box was packed. Mabel, Maurice's kiddy sister, cried over everything as it was put in. It was a very wet day.

'If it had been any school but old Strong's,' she sobbed.

She and her brother knew that school well: its windows, dulled with wire blinds, its big alarm bell, the high walls of its grounds, bristling with spikes, the iron gates, always locked, through which gloomy boys, imprisoned, scowled on a free world. Dr Strong-itharm's was a school 'for backward and difficult boys'. Need I say more?

Well, there was no help for it. The box was packed, the cab was at the door. The farewells had been said. Maurice determined that he wouldn't cry and he didn't, which gave him the one touch of pride and joy that such a scene could yield. Then at the last moment, just as father had one leg in the cab, the Taxes called. Father went back into the house to write a cheque. Mother and Mabel had retired in tears. Maurice used the reprieve to go back after his postage-stamp album. Already he was planning how to impress the other boys at old Strong's, and his was really a very fair collection. He ran up into the schoolroom, expecting to find it empty. But some one was there: Lord Hugh, in the very middle of the ink-stained table-cloth.

'You brute,' said Maurice; 'you know jolly well I'm going away, or you wouldn't be here.' And, indeed, the room had never, somehow, been a favourite of Lord Hugh's.

'Meaow,' said Lord Hugh.

'Mew!' said Maurice, with scorn. 'That's what you always say. All that fuss about a jolly little sardine-tin. Anyone would have thought you'd be only too glad to have it to play with. I wonder how you'd like being a boy? Lickings, and lessons, and impots, and sent back from breakfast to wash your ears. You wash yours anywhere—I wonder what they'd say to me if I washed my ears on the drawing-room hearthrug?'

'Meaow,' said Lord Hugh, and washed an ear, as though he were showing off.

'Mew,' said Maurice again; 'that's all you can say.'

'Oh, no, it isn't,' said Lord Hugh, and stopped his ear-washing.

'I say!' said Maurice in awestruck tones.

'If you think cats have such a jolly time,' said Lord Hugh, 'why not *be* a cat?'

'I would if I could,' said Maurice, 'and fight you—'

'Thank you,' said Lord Hugh.

'But I can't,' said Maurice.

'Oh, yes, you can,' said Lord Hugh. 'You've only got to say the word.'

'What word?'

Lord Hugh told him the word; but I will not tell you, for fear you should say it by accident and then be sorry.

'And if I say that, I shall turn into a cat?'

'Of course,' said the cat.

'Oh, yes, I see,' said Maurice. 'But I'm not taking any, thanks. I don't want to be a cat for always.'

'You needn't,' said Lord Hugh. 'You've only got to get some one to say to you, "Please leave off being a cat and be Maurice again," and there you are.'

Maurice thought of Dr Strongitharm's. He also thought of the horror of his father when he should find Maurice gone, vanished, not to be traced. 'He'll be sorry, then.' Maurice told himself, and to the cat he said, suddenly:—

'Right—I'll do it. What's the word, again?'

'—,' said the cat.

'—,' said Maurice; and suddenly the table shot up to the height of a house, the walls to the height of tenement buildings, the pattern on the carpet became enormous, and Maurice found himself on all fours. He tried to stand up on his feet, but his shoulders were oddly heavy. He could only rear himself upright for a moment, and then fell heavily on his hands. He looked down at them; they seemed to have grown shorter and fatter, and were encased in black fur gloves. He felt a desire to walk on all fours— tried it—did it. It was very odd—the movement of the arms straight from the shoulder, more like the movement of the piston of an engine than anything Maurice could think of at that moment.

'I am asleep,' said Maurice—'I am dreaming this. I am dreaming I am a cat. I hope I dreamed that about the sardine-tin and Lord Hugh's tail, and Dr Strong's.'

'You didn't,' said a voice he knew and yet didn't know, 'and you aren't dreaming this.'

'Yes, I am,' said Maurice; 'and now I'm going to dream that I fight that beastly black cat, and give him the best licking he ever had in his life. Come on, Lord Hugh.'

A loud laugh answered him.

'Excuse me smiling,' said the voice he knew and didn't know, 'but don't you see—you *are* Lord Hugh!'

A great hand picked Maurice up from the floor and held him in the air. He felt the position to be not only undignified but unsafe, and gave himself a shake of mingled relief and resentment when the hand set him down on the inky table-cloth.

'You are Lord Hugh now, my dear Maurice,' said the voice, and a huge face came quite close to his. It was his own face, as it would have seemed through a magnifying glass. And the voice—oh, horror!—the voice was his own—Maurice Basingstoke's voice. Maurice shrank from the voice, and he would have liked to claw the face, but he had had no practice.

'You are Lord Hugh,' the voice repeated, 'and I am Maurice. I like being Maurice. I am so large and strong. I could drown you in the water-butt, my poor cat—oh, so easily. No, don't spit and swear. It's bad manners—even in a cat.'

'Maurice!' shouted Mr Basingstoke from between the door and the cab.

Maurice, from habit, leaped towards the door.

'It's no use *your* going,' said the thing that looked like a giant reflection of Maurice: 'it's *me* he wants.'

'But I didn't agree to your being me.'

'That's poetry, even if it isn't grammar,' said the thing that looked like Maurice. 'Why, my good cat, don't you see that if you are I, I must be you? Otherwise we should interfere with time and space, upset the balance of power, and as likely as not destroy the solar system. Oh, yes—I'm you, right enough, and shall be, till some one tells you to change from Lord Hugh into Maurice. And now you've got to find some one to do it.'

('Maurice!' thundered the voice of Mr Basingstoke.)

'That'll be easy enough,' said Maurice.

'Think so?' said the other.

'But I shan't try yet. I want to have some fun first. I shall catch heaps of mice!'

'Think so? You forget that your whiskers are cut off—Maurice cut them. Without whiskers, how can you judge of the width of the places you go through? Take care you don't get stuck in a hole that you can't get out of or go in through, my good cat.'

'Don't call me a cat,' said Maurice, and felt that his tail was growing thick and angry.

'You *are* a cat, you know—and that little bit of temper that I see in your tail reminds me—'

Maurice felt himself gripped round the middle, abruptly lifted, and carried swiftly through the air. The quickness of the movement made him giddy. The light went so quickly past him that it might as well have been darkness. He saw nothing, felt nothing, except a sort of long sea-sickness, and then suddenly he was not being moved. He could see now. He could feel. He was being held tight in a sort of vice—a vice covered with chequered cloth. It looked like the pattern, very much exaggerated, of his school knickerbockers. It *was*. He was being held between the hard, relentless knees of that creature that had once been Lord Hugh, and to whose tail he had tied a sardine-tin. Now *he* was Lord H gh, and something was being tied to *his* tail. Something mysterious, terrible. Very well, he would show that he was not afraid of anything that could be attached to tails. The string rubbed his fur the wrong way—it was that that annoyed him, not the string itself; and as for what was at the end of the string, what *could* that matter to any sensible cat? Maurice was quite decided that he was—and would keep on being—a sensible cat.

The string, however, and the uncomfortable, tight position between those chequered knees—something or other was getting on his nerves.

'Maurice!' shouted his father below, and the be-catted Maurice bounded between the knees of the creature that wore his clothes and his looks.

'Coming, father,' this thing called, and sped away, leaving Maurice on the servant's bed—under which Lord Hugh had taken refuge, with his tin-can, so short and yet so long a time ago. The stairs re-echoed to the loud boots which Maurice had never before thought loud; he had often, indeed, wondered that any one could object to them. He wondered now no longer.

He heard the front door slam. That thing had gone to Dr

Strongitharm's. That was one comfort. Lord Hugh was a boy now; he would know what it was to be a boy. He, Maurice, was a cat, and he meant to taste fully all catty pleasures, from milk to mice. Meanwhile he was without mice or milk, and, unaccustomed as he was to a tail, he could not but feel that all was not right with his own. There was a feeling of weight, a feeling of discomfort, of positive terror. If he should move, what would that thing that was tied to his tail do? Rattle, of course. Oh, but he could not bear it if that thing rattled. Nonsense; it was only a sardine-tin. Yes, Maurice knew that. But all the same—if it did rattle! He moved his tail the least little soft inch. No sound. Perhaps really there wasn't anything tied to his tail. But he couldn't be sure unless he moved. But if he moved the thing would rattle, and if it rattled Maurice felt sure that he would expire or go mad. A mad cat. What a dreadful thing to be! Yet he couldn't sit on that bed for ever, waiting, waiting, waiting for the dreadful thing to happen.

'Oh, dear,' sighed Maurice the cat. 'I never knew what people meant by "afraid" before.'

His cat-heart was beating heavily against his furry side. His limbs were getting cramped—he must move. He did. And instantly the awful thing happened. The sardine-tin touched the iron of the bedfoot. It rattled.

'Oh, I can't bear it, I can't,' cried poor Maurice, in a heartrending meaow that echoed through the house. He leaped from the bed and tore through the door and down the stairs, and behind him came the most terrible thing in the world. People might call it a sardine-tin, but he knew better. It was the soul of all the fear that ever had been or ever could be. *It rattled*.

Maurice who was a cat flew down the stairs; down, down—the rattling followed. Oh, horrible! Down, down! At the foot of the stairs the horror, caught by something—a banister—a stair-rod— stopped. The string on Maurice's tail tightened, his tail was jerked, he was stopped. But the noise had stopped too. Maurice lay only just alive at the foot of the stairs.

It was Mabel who untied the string and soothed his terrors with strokings and tender love-words. Maurice was surprised to find what a nice little girl his sister really was.

'I'll never tease you again,' he tried to say, softly—but that was not what he said. What he said was 'Purrr.'

'Dear pussy, nice poor pussy, then,' said Mabel, and she hid away the sardine-tin and did not tell any one. This seemed unjust to Maurice until he remembered that, of course, Mabel thought that he was really Lord Hugh, and that the person who had tied the tin to his tail was her brother Maurice. Then he was half grateful. She carried him down, in soft, safe arms, to the kitchen, and asked cook to give him some milk.

'Tell me to change back into Maurice,' said Maurice who was quite worn out by his cattish experiences. But no one heard him. What they heard was, 'Meaow—Meaow—Meeeaow!'

Then Maurice saw how he had been tricked. He could be changed back into a boy as soon as any one said to him, 'Leave off being a cat and be Maurice again,' but his tongue had no longer the power to ask any one to say it.

He did not sleep well that night. For one thing he was not accustomed to sleeping on the kitchen hearthrug, and the black-beetles were too many and too cordial. He was glad when cook came down and turned him out into the garden, where the Oct-ober frost still lay white on the yellowed stalks of sunflowers and nasturtiums. He took a walk, climbed a tree, failed to catch a bird, and felt better. He began also to feel hungry. A delicious scent came stealing out of the back kitchen door. Oh, joy, there were to be herrings for breakfast! Maurice hastened in and took his place on his usual chair.

His mother said, 'Down, puss,' and gently tilted the chair so that Maurice fell off it. Then the family had herrings. Maurice said, 'You might give me some,' and he said it so often that his father, who, of course, heard only mewings, said:—

'For goodness' sake put that cat out of the room.'

Maurice breakfasted later, in the dust-bin, on herring heads.

But he kept himself up with a new and splendid idea. They would give him milk presently, and then they should see.

He spent the afternoon sitting on the sofa in the dining-room, listening to the conversation of his father and mother. It is said that listeners never heard any good of themselves. He heard his father say that he was a fine, plucky little chap, but he needed a severe lesson, and Dr Strongitharm was the man to give it to him. He heard his mother say things that made his heart throb in his throat and the tears prick behind those green cat-eyes of his. He had always thought his parents a little bit unjust. Now they did him so much more than justice that he felt quite small and mean inside his cat-skin.

'He's a dear, good, affectionate boy,' said mother. 'It's only his high spirits. Don't you think, darling, perhaps you were a little hard on him?'

'It was for his own good,' said father.

'Of course,' said mother; 'but I can't bear to think of him at that dreadful school.'

'Well—,' father was beginning, when Jane came in with the tea-things on a clattering tray, whose sound made Maurice tremble in every leg. Father and mother began to talk about the weather.

Maurice felt very affectionately to both his parents. The natural way of showing this was to jump on to the sideboard and thence on to his father's shoulders. He landed there on his four padded feet, light as a feather, but father was not pleased.

'Bother the cat!' he cried. 'Jane, put it out of the room.'

Maurice was put out. His great idea, which was to be carried out with milk, would certainly not be carried out in the dining-room. He sought the kitchen, and, seeing a milk-can on the window-ledge, jumped up beside the can and patted it as he had seen Lord Hugh do.

'My!' said a friend of Jane's who happened to be there, 'ain't that cat clever—a perfect moral, I call her.'

'He's nothing to boast of this time,' said cook. 'I will say for Lord Hugh he's not often taken in with a empty can.'

This was naturally mortifying for Maurice, but he pretended not to hear, and jumped from the window to the tea-table and patted the milk-jug.

'Come,' said the cook, 'that's more like it,' and she poured him out a full saucer and set it on the floor.

Now was the chance Maurice had longed for. Now he could carry out that idea of his. He was very thirsty, for he had had nothing since that delicious breakfast in the dust-bin. But not for worlds would he have drunk the milk. No. He carefully dipped his right paw in it, for his idea was to make letters with it, on the kitchen oil-cloth. He meant to write: 'Please tell me to leave off being a cat and be Maurice again,' but he found his paw a very clumsy pen, and he had to rub out the first 'P' because it only looked like an accident. Then he tried again and actually did make a 'P' that any fairminded person could have read quite easily.

'I wish they'd notice,' he said, and before he got the 'I' written they did notice.

'Drat the cat,' said the cook; 'look how he's messing the floor up.'

And she took away the milk.

Maurice put pride aside and mewed to have the milk put down again. But he did not get it.

Very weary, very thirsty, and very tired of being Lord Hugh, he presently found his way to the schoolroom, where Mabel with patient toil was doing her home-lessons. She took him on her lap and stroked him while she learned her French verb. He felt that he was growing very fond of her. People were quite right to be kind to dumb animals. Presently she had to stop stroking him and do a map. And after that she kissed him and put him down and went away. All the time she had been doing the map, Maurice had had but one thought: *Ink!*

The moment the door had closed behind her—how sensible people were who closed doors gently—he stood up in her chair with one paw on the map and the other on the ink. Unfortunately, the inkstand top was made to dip pens in, and not to dip paws. But Maurice was desperate. He deliberately upset the ink—most of it rolled over the table-cloth and fell pattering on the carpet, but with what was left he wrote quite plainly, across the map:—

'Please tell Lord Hugh
to stop being
a cat and be Mau
rice again.'

'There!' he said; 'they can't make any mistake about that.' They didn't. But they made a mistake about who had done it, and Mabel was deprived of jam with her supper bread.

Her assurance that some naughty boy must have come through the window and done it while she was not there convinced no-body, and, indeed, the window was shut and bolted.

Maurice, wild with indignation, did not mend matters by seizing the opportunity of a few minutes' solitude to write:

'It was not Mabel
it was Maur
ice I mean Lord Hugh,

because when that was seen Mabel was instantly sent to bed.

'It's not fair!' cried Maurice.

'My dear,' said Maurice's father, 'if that cat goes on mewing to this extent you'll have to get rid of it.'

Maurice said not another word. It was bad enough to be a cat, but to be a cat that was 'got rid of'! He knew how people got rid of cats. In a stricken silence he left the room and slunk up the stairs—he dared not mew again, even at the door of Mabel's room. But when Jane went in to put Mabel's light out Maurice crept in too, and in the dark tried with stifled mews and purrs to explain to Mabel how sorry he was. Mabel stroked him and he went to sleep, his last waking thought amazement at the blindness that had once made him call her a silly little kid.

If you have ever been a cat you will understand something of what Maurice endured during the dreadful days that followed. If you have not, I can never make you understand fully. There was the affair of the fishmonger's tray balanced on the wall by the back door—the delicious curled-up whiting; Maurice knew as well as you do that one mustn't steal fish out of other people's trays, but the cat that he was didn't know. There was an inward struggle —and Maurice was beaten by the cat-nature. Later he was beaten by the cook.

Then there was that very painful incident with the butcher's dog, the flight across the gardens, the safety of the plum tree gained only just in time.

And worst of all, despair took hold of him, for he saw that nothing he could do would make any one say those simple words that would release him. He had hoped that Mabel might at last be made to understand, but the ink had failed him; she did not understand his subdued mewings, and when he got the cardboard letters and made the same sentence with them Mabel only thought it was that naughty boy who came through locked windows. Somehow he could not spell before any one—his nerves were not what they had been. His brain now gave him no new ideas. He felt that he was really growing like a cat in his mind. His interest in his meals grew beyond even what it had been when they were a schoolboy's meals. He hunted mice with growing enthusiasm, though the loss of his whiskers to measure narrow places with made hunting difficult.

He grew expert in bird-stalking, and often got quite near to a bird before it flew away, laughing at him. But all the time, in his heart, he was very, very miserable. And so the week went by.

Maurice in his cat shape dreaded more and more the time when Lord Hugh in the boy shape should come back from Dr Strongitharm's. He knew—who better?—exactly the kind of things boys do to cats, and he trembled to the end of his handsome half-Persian tail.

And then the boy came home from Dr Strongitharm's, and at the first sound of his boots in the hall Maurice in the cat's body fled with silent haste to hide in the boot-cupboard.

Here, ten minutes later, the boy that had come back from Dr

Strongitharm's found him.

Maurice fluffed up his tail and unsheathed his claws. Whatever this boy was going to do to him Maurice meant to resist, and his resistance should hurt the boy as much as possible. I am sorry to say Maurice swore softly among the boots, but cat-swearing is not really wrong.

'Come out, you old duffer,' said Lord Hugh in the boy shape of Maurice. 'I'm not going to hurt you.'

'I'll see to that,' said Maurice, backing into the corner, all teeth and claws.

'Oh, I've had such a time!' said Lord Hugh. 'It's no use, you know, old chap; I can see where you are by your green eyes. My word, they do shine. I've been caned and shut up in a dark room and given thousands of lines to write out.'

'I've been beaten, too, if you come to that,' mewed Maurice. 'Besides the butcher's dog.'

It was an intense relief to speak to someone who could understand his mews.

'Well, I suppose it's Pax for the future,' said Lord Hugh; 'if you won't come out, you won't. Please leave off being a cat and be Maurice again.'

And instantly Maurice, admid a heap of goloshes and old tennis bats, felt with a swelling heart that he was no longer a cat. No more of those undignified four legs, those tiresome pointed ears, so difficult to wash, that furry coat, that contemptible tail, and that terrible inability to express all one's feelings in two words— 'mew' and 'purr'.

He scrambled out of the cupboard, and the boots and goloshes fell off him like spray off a bather.

He stood upright in those very chequered knickerbockers that were so terrible when their knees held one vice-like, while things were tied to one's tail. He was face to face with another boy, exactly like himself.

'*You* haven't changed, then—but there can't be two Maurices.'

'There shan't be; not if I know it,' said the other boy; 'a boy's life is a dog's life. Quick, before any one comes.'

'Quick what?' asked Maurice.

'Why, tell me to leave off being a boy, and to be Lord Hugh Cecil again.'

Maurice told him at once. And at once the boy was gone, and there was Lord Hugh in his own shape, purring politely, yet with a watchful eye on Maurice's movements.

'Oh, you needn't be afraid, old chap. It's Pax right enough,' Maurice murmured in the ear of Lord Hugh. And Lord Hugh, arching his back under Maurice's stroking hand, replied with a purrrr-meaow that spoke volumes.

'Oh, Maurice, here you are. It *is* nice of you to be nice to Lord Hugh, when it was because of him you—'

'He's a good old chap,' said Maurice, carelessly. 'And you're not half a bad old girl. See?'

Mabel almost wept for joy at this magnificent compliment, and Lord Hugh himself took on a more happy and confident air.

Please dismiss any fears which you may entertain that after this Maurice became a model boy. He didn't. But he was much nicer than before. The conversation which he overheard when he was a cat makes him more patient with his father and mother. And he is almost always nice to Mabel, for he cannot forget all that she was to him when he wore the shape of Lord Hugh. His father attributes all the improvement in his son's character to that week at Dr Strongitharm's—which, as you know, Maurice never had. Lord Hugh's character is unchanged. Cats learn slowly and with difficulty.

Only Maurice and Lord Hugh know the truth—Maurice has never told it to any one except me, and Lord Hugh is a very reserved cat. He never at any time had that free flow of mew which distinguished and endangered the cat-hood of Maurice.

Charles

The day Laurie started kindergarten he renounced corduroy overalls with bibs and began wearing blue jeans with a belt; I watched him go off the first morning with the older girl next door, seeing clearly that an era of my life was ended, my sweet-voiced nursery-school tot replaced by a long-trousered, swaggering character who forgot to stop at the corner and wave goodbye to me.

He came home the same way, the front door slamming open, his cap on the floor, and the voice suddenly became raucous shouting, 'Isn't anybody *here*?'

At lunch he spoke insolently to his father, spilled Jannie's milk and remarked that his teacher said that we were not to take the name of the Lord in vain.

'How was school today?' I asked, elaborately casual.

'All right,' he said.

'Did you learn anything?' his father asked.

Laurie regarded his father coldly. 'I didn't learn nothing,' he said.

'Anything,' I said. 'Didn't learn anything.'

'The teacher spanked a boy, though.' Laurie said, addressing his bread and butter. 'For being fresh,' he added with his mouth full.

'What did he do?' I asked. 'Who was it?'

Laurie thought. 'It was Charles,' he said. 'He was fresh. The teacher spanked him and made him stand in a corner. He was awfully fresh.'

'What did he do?' I asked again, but Laurie slid off his chair, took a cookie, and left, while his father was still saying, 'See here, young man.'

The next day Laurie remarked at lunch, as soon as he sat down, 'Well, Charles was bad again today.' He grinned enormously and said, 'Today Charles hit the teacher.'

'Good heavens,' I said, mindful of the Lord's name. 'I suppose he got spanked again?'

'He sure did,' Laurie said. 'Look up,' he said to his father.

'What?' his father said, looking up.

'Look down,' Laurie said. 'Look at my thumb. Gee, you're dumb.' He began to laugh insanely.

'Why did Charles hit the teacher?' I asked quickly.

'Because she tried to make him colour with red crayons,' Laurie said. 'Charles wanted to colour with green crayons so he hit the teacher and she spanked him and said nobody play with Charles but everybody did.'

The third day—it was Wednesday of the first week—Charles bounced a seesaw onto the head of a little girl and made her bleed and the teacher made him stay inside all during recess. Thursday Charles had to stand in a corner during storytime because he kept pounding his feet on the floor. Friday Charles was deprived of blackboard privileges because he threw chalk.

On Saturday I remarked to my husband, 'Do you think kindergarten is too unsettling for Laurie? All this toughness and bad grammar, and this Charles boy sounds like such a bad influence.'

'It'll be all right,' my husband said reassuringly. Bound to be people like Charles in the world. Might as well meet them now as later.'

On Monday Laurie came home late, full of news. 'Charles,' he shouted as he came up the hill; I was waiting anxiously on the front steps; 'Charles,' Laurie yelled all the way up the hill, 'Charles was bad again.'

'Come right in,' I said, as soon as he came close enough. 'Lunch is waiting.'

'You know what Charles did?' he demanded, following me through the door. 'Charles yelled so in school they sent a boy in from first grade to tell the teacher she had to make Charles keep quiet, and so Charles had to stay after school. And so all the children stayed to watch him.'

'What did he do?' I asked.

'He just sat there,' Laurie said, climbing into his chair at the table. 'Hi Pop, y'old dust mop.'

'Charles had to stay after school today,' I told my husband. 'Everyone stayed with him.'

'What does this Charles look like?' my husband asked Laurie. 'What's his other name?'

'He's bigger than me,' Laurie said. 'And he doesn't have any rubbers and he doesn't ever wear a jacket.'

Monday night was the first Parent-Teachers meeting, and only the fact that Jannie had a cold kept me from going; I wanted passionately to meet Charles' mother. On Tuesday Laurie remarked suddenly. 'Our teacher had a friend come see her in school today.'

'Charles' mother?' my husband and I asked simultaneously.

'Naaah,' Laurie said scornfully. 'It was a man who came and made us do exercises. Look.' He climbed down from his chair and squatted down and touched his toes. 'Like this,' he said. He got solemnly back into his chair and said, picking up his fork, 'Charles didn't even *do* exercises.'

'That's fine,' I said heartily. 'Didn't Charles want to do exercises?'

'Naaah,' Laurie said. 'Charles was so fresh to the teacher's friend he wasn't *let* do exercises.'

'Fresh again?' I said.

'He kicked the teacher's friend,' Laurie said. 'The teacher's friend told Charles to touch his toes like I just did and Charles kicked him.'

'What are they going to do about Charles, do you suppose?' Laurie's father asked him.

Laurie shrugged elaborately. 'Throw him out of the school, I guess,' he said.

Wednesday and Thursday were routine; Charles yelled during story hour and hit a boy in the stomach and made him cry. On Friday Charles stayed after school again and so did all the other children.

With the third week of kindergarten Charles was an institution in our family; Jannie was being a Charles when she cried all afternoon; Laurie did a Charles when he filled his wagon full of mud and pulled it through the kitchen; even my husband, when he caught his elbow in the telephone cord and pulled telephone, ash tray, and a bowl of flowers off the table, said, after the first minute, 'Looks like Charles.'

During the third and fourth weeks there seemed to be a reformation in Charles; Laurie reported grimly at lunch on Thursday of the third week, 'Charles was so good today the teacher gave him an apple.'

'What?' I said, and my husband added warily, 'You mean Charles?'

'Charles,' Laurie said. 'He gave the crayons around and he picked up the books afterward and the teacher said he was her helper.'

'What happened?' I asked incredulously.

'He was her helper, that's all,' Laurie said, and shrugged.

'Can this be true, about Charles?' I asked my husband that night. 'Can something like this happen?'

'Wait and see,' my husband said cynically. 'When you've got a Charles to deal with, this may mean he's only plotting.'

He seemed to be wrong. For over a week Charles was the teacher's helper; each day he handed things out and he picked things up; no-one had to stay after school.

'The PTA meeting's next week again,' I told my husband one evening. 'I'm going to find Charles' mother there.'

'Ask her what happened to Charles,' my husband said. 'I'd like to know.'

On Friday of that week things were back to normal. 'You know what Charles did today?' Laurie demanded at the lunch table, in a voice slightly awed. 'He told a little girl to say a word and she said it and the teacher washed her mouth out with soap and Charles laughed.'

'What word?' his father asked unwisely, and Laurie said, 'I'll have to whisper it to you, it's so bad.' He got down off his chair and went around to his father. His father bent his head down and Laurie whispered joyfully. His father's eyes widened.

'Did Charles tell the little girl to say *that*?' he asked respectfully.

'She said it *twice*,' Laurie said. 'Charles told her to say it *twice*.'

'What happened to Charles?' my husband asked.

'Nothing,' Laurie said. 'He was passing out the crayons.'

Monday morning Charles abandoned the little girl and said the evil word himself three or four times, getting his mouth washed out with soap each time. He also threw chalk.

My husband came to the door with me that evening as I set out for the PTA meeting. 'Invite her over for a cup of tea after the meeting,' he said. 'I want to get a look at her.'

'If only she's there,' I said prayerfully.

'She'll be there,' my husband said. 'I don't see how they could hold a PTA meeting without Charles' mother.'

At the meeting I sat restlessly, scanning each comfortable matronly face, trying to determine which one hid the secret of Charles. None of them looked to me haggard enough. No-one stood up in the meeting and apologized for the way her son had been acting. No-one mentioned Charles.

After the meeting I identified and sought out Laurie's kindergarten teacher. She had a plate with a cup of tea and a piece of chocolate cake; I had a plate with a cup of tea and a piece of marshmallow cake. We manoeuvred up to one another cautiously and smiled.

'I've been so anxious to meet you,' I said. 'I'm Laurie's mother.'

'We're all so interested in Laurie,' she said.

'Well, he certainly likes kindergarten,' I said. 'He talks about it all the time.'

'We had a little trouble adjusting, the first week or so,' she said primly, 'but now he's a fine little helper. With lapses, of course.'

'Laurie usually adjusts very quickly,' I said. 'I suppose this time it's Charles' influence.'

'Charles?'

'Yes,' I said, laughing, 'you must have your hands full in that kindergarten, with Charles.'

'Charles?' she said. 'We don't have any Charles in the kindergarten.'

Edgar Allan Poe

A Tale of the Ragged Mountains

During the autumn of the year 1827, while residing near Charlottesville, Virginia, I casually made the acquaintance of Mr Augustus Bedloe. This young gentleman was remarkable in every respect, and excited in me a profound interest and curiosity. I found it impossible to comprehend him either in his moral or his physical relations. Of his family I could obtain no satisfactory account. Whence he came, I never ascertained. Even about his age—although I call him a young gentleman— there was something which perplexed me in no little degree. He certainly *seemed* young—and he made a point of speaking about his youth—yet there were moments when I should have had little trouble in imagining him a hundred years of age. But in no regard was he more peculiar than in his personal appearance. He was singularly tall and thin. He stooped much. His limbs were exceedingly long and emaciated. His forehead was broad and low. His complexion was absolutely bloodless. His mouth was large and flexible, and his teeth were more wildly uneven, although sound, than I had ever before seen teeth in a human head. The expression of his smile, however, was by no means unpleasing, as might be supposed; but it had no variation whatever. It was one of profound melancholy—of a phaseless and unceasing gloom. His eyes were abnormally large, and round like those of a cat. The pupils, too, upon any accession or diminution of light, underwent contraction or dilation, just such as is observed in the feline tribe. In moments of excitement the orbs grew bright to a degree almost inconceivable; seeming to emit luminous rays, not of a reflected but of an intrinsic lustre, as does a candle or the sun; yet their ordinary condition was so totally vapid, filmy, and dull, as to convey the idea of the eyes of a long-interred corpse.

These peculiarities of person appeared to cause him much annoyance, and he was continually alluding to them in a sort of half explanatory, half apologetic strain, which, when I first heard it, impressed me very painfully. I soon, however, grew accustomed to it, and my uneasiness wore off. It seemed to be his design rather to insinuate than directly to assert that, physically, he had not always been what he was—that a long series of neuralgic attacks had reduced him from a condition of more than usual personal beauty, to that which I saw. For many years past he had been attended by a physician, named Templeton—an old gentleman, perhaps seventy years of age—whom he had first encountered at Saratoga, and from whose attention, while there, he either received, or fancied that he received, great benefit. The result was that Bedloe, who was wealthy, had made an arrangement with Dr Templeton, by which the latter, in consideration of a liberal annual allowance, had consented to devote his time and medical experience exclusively to the care of the invalid.

Doctor Templeton had been a traveller in his younger days, and at Paris had become a convert, in great measure, to the doctrine of Mesmer. It was altogether by means of magnetic remedies that he had succeeded in alleviating the acute pains of his patient; and this success had very naturally inspired the latter with a certain degree of confidence in the opinions from which the remedies had been educed. The doctor, however, like all enthusiasts, had struggled hard to make a thorough convert of his pupil, and finally so far gained his point as to induce the sufferer to submit to numerous experiments. By a frequent repetition of these, a result had arisen, which of late days has become so common as to attract little or no attention, but which, at the period of which I write, had very rarely been known in America. I mean to say, that between Dr Templeton and Bedloe there had grown up, little by little, a very distinct and strongly-marked *rapport*, or magnetic relation. I am not prepared to assert, however, that this *rapport* extended beyond the limits of the simple sleep-producing power; but this power itself had attained great intensity. At the first attempt to induce the magnetic somnolency, the mesmerist entirely failed. In the fifth or sixth he succeeded very partially, and after long-continued effort. Only at the twelfth was the triumph complete. After this the will of the patient succumbed rapidly to that of the physician, so that, when I first became acquainted with the two, sleep was brought about almost instantaneously by the mere volition of the operator, even when the invalid was unaware of his presence. It is only now, in the year 1845, when similar miracles are witnessed daily by thousands, that I dare venture to record this apparent impossiblity as a matter of serious fact.   —

The temperament of Bedloe was in the highest degree sensitive, excitable, enthusiastic. His imagination was singularly vigorous and creative; and no doubt it derived additional force from the habitual use of morphine, which he swallowed in great quantity, and without which he would have found it impossible to exist. It was his practice to take a very large dose of it immediately after breakfast each morning,—or, rather, immediately after a cup of strong coffee, for he ate nothing in the forenoon,—and then set forth alone, or attended only by a dog, upon a long ramble among the chain of wild and dreary hills that lie westward and southward of Charlottesville, and are there dignified by the title of the Ragged Mountains.

Upon a dim, warm, misty day, toward the close of November, and during the strange *interregnum* of the seasons which in America is termed the Indian summer, Mr Bedloe departed as usual for the hills. The day passed, and still he did not return.

About eight o'clock at night, having become seriously alarmed at his protracted absence, we were about setting out in search of him, when he unexpectedly made his appearance, in health no worse than usual, and in rather more than ordinary spirits. The account which he gave of his expedition, and of the events which had detained him, was a singular one indeed.

'You will remember,' said he, 'that it was about nine in the morning when I left Charlottesville. I bent my steps immediately to the mountains, and, about ten, entered a gorge which was entirely new to me. I followed the windings of this pass with much interest. The scenery which presented itself on all sides, although scarcely entitled to be called grand, had about it an indescribable and to me a delicious aspect of dreary desolation. The solitude seemed absolutely virgin. I could not help believing that the green sods and the grey rocks upon which I trod had been trodden never before by the foot of a human being. So entirely secluded, and in fact inaccessible, except through a series of accidents, is the entrance of the ravine, that it is by no means impossible that I was the first adventurer—the very first and sole adventurer who had ever penetrated its recesses.

'The thick and peculiar mist, or smoke, which distinguishes the Indian summer, and which now hung heavily over all objects served, no doubt, to deepen the vague impressions which these objects created. So dense was this pleasant fog that I could at no time see more than a dozen yards of the path before me. This path was excessively sinuous, and as the sun could not be seen, I soon lost all idea of the direction in which I journeyed. In the meantime the morphine had its customary effect—that of enduing all the external world with an intensity of interest. In the quivering of a leaf—in the hue of a blade of grass—in the shape of a trefoil—in the humming of a bee—in the gleaming of a dewdrop—in the breathing of the wind—in the faint odours that came from the forest—there came a whole universe of suggestion—a gay and motley train of rhapsodical and immethodical thought.

'Busied in this, I walked on for several hours, during which the mist deepened around me to so great an extent that at length I was reduced to an absolute groping of the way. And now an indescribable uneasiness possessed me—a species of nervous hesitation and tremor. I feared to tread, lest I should be precipitated into some abyss. I remembered, too, strange stories told about these Ragged Hills, and of the uncouth and fierce races of men who tenanted their groves and caverns. A thousand vague fancies oppressed and disconcerted me—fancies the more distressing because vague. Very suddenly my attention was arrested by the loud beating of a drum.

'My amazement was, of course, extreme. A drum in these hills was a thing unknown. I could not have been more surprised at the sound of the trump of the Archangel. But a new and still more astounding source of interest and perplexity arose. There came a wild rattling or jingling sound, as if of a bunch of large keys, and upon the instant a dusky-visaged and half-naked man rushed past me with a shriek. He came so close to my person that I felt his hot breath upon my face. He bore in one hand an instrument composed of an assemblage of steel rings, and shook them vigorously as he ran. Scarcely had he disappeared in the mist, before, panting after him, with open mouth and glaring eyes, there darted a huge beast. I could not be mistaken in its character. It was a hyena.

'The sight of this monster rather relieved than heightened my terrors—for I now made sure that I dreamed, and endeavoured to arouse myself to waking consciousness. I stepped boldly and briskly forward. I rubbed my eyes. I called aloud. I pinched my limbs. A small spring of water presented itself to my view, and here, stooping, I bathed my hands and my head and neck. This seemed to dissipate the equivocal sensations which had hitherto annoyed me. I arose, as I thought, a new man, and proceeded steadily and complacently on my unknown way.

'At length, quite overcome by exertion, and by a certain oppressive closeness of the atmosphere, I seated myself beneath a tree. Presently there came a feeble gleam of sunshine, and the shadow of the leaves of the tree fell faintly but definitely upon the grass. At this shadow I gazed wonderingly for many minutes. Its character stupefied me with astonishment. I looked upward. The tree was a palm.

'I now rose hurriedly, and in a state of fearful agitation—for the fancy that I dreamed would serve me no longer. I saw—I felt that I had perfect command of my senses—and these senses now brought to my soul a world of novel and singular sensation. The heat became all at once intolerable. A strange odour loaded the breeze. A low, continuous murmur, like that arising from a full, but gently flowing river, came to my ears, intermingled with the peculiar hum of multitudinous human voices.

'While I listened in an extremity of astonishment which I need not attempt to describe, a strong and brief gust of wind bore off the incumbent fog as if by the wand of an enchanter.

'I found myself at the foot of a high mountain, and looking down into a vast plain, through which wound a majestic river. On the margin of this river stood an Eastern-looking city, such as we read of in the Arabian Tales, but of a character even more singular than any there described. From my position, which was far above the level of the town. I could perceive its every nook and corner, as if delineated on a map. The streets seemed innumerable, and crossed each other irregularly in all directions, but were rather long winding alleys than streets, and absolutely swarmed with inhabitants. The houses were wildly picturesque. On every hand was a wilderness of balconies, of verandas, of minarets, of shrines, and fantastically carved oriels. Bazaars abounded; and there were displayed rich wares in infinite variety and profusion—silks, muslins, the most dazzling cutlery, the most magnificent jewels and gems. Besides these things, were seen, on all sides, banners and palanquins, litters with stately dames close-veiled, elephants gorgeously caparisoned, idols grotesquely hewn, drums, banners, and gongs, spears, silver and gilded maces. And amid the crowd, and the clamour and the general intricacy and confusion—amid the million of black and yellow men, turbaned and robed, and of flowing beard, there roamed a countless multitude of holy filleted bulls, while vast legions of the filthy but sacred ape clambered, chattering and shrieking, about the cornices of the mosques, or clung to the minarets and oriels. From the swarming streets to the banks of the river, there descended innumerable flights of steps leading to bathing places, while the river itself seemed to force a passage with difficulty through the vast fleets of deeply burdened ships that far and wide encountered its surface. Beyond the limits of the city arose, in frequent majestic groups, the palm and the cocoa, with other gigantic and weird trees of vast age; and here and there might be seen a field of rice, the thatched hut of a peasant, a tank, a stray temple, a gipsy camp, or a solitary graceful maiden taking her way, with a pitcher upon her head, to the banks of the magnificent river.

'You will say now, of course, that I dreamed; but not so. What I saw—what I heard—what I felt—what I thought—had about it nothing of the unmistakable idiosyncrasy of the dream. All was rigorously self-consistent. At first, doubting that I was really awake, I entered into a series of tests, which soon convinced me that I really was. Now when one dreams, and, in the dream, suspects that he dreams, the suspicion *never fails to confirm itself*, and the sleeper is almost immediately aroused. Thus Novalis errs not in saying that "we are near waking when we dream that we dream." Had the vision occurred to me as I describe it, without my suspecting it as a dream, then a dream it might absolutely have been, but, occurring as it did, and suspected and tested as it was, I am forced to class it among other phenomena.'

'In this I am not sure that you are wrong,' observed Dr Templeton, 'but proceed. You arose and descended into the city.'

'I arose,' continued Bedloe, regarding the Doctor with an air of profound astonishment. 'I arose as you say, and descended into the city. On my ways I fell in with an immense populace, crowding through every avenue, all in the same direction, and exhibiting in every action the wildest excitement. Very suddenly, and by some inconceivable impulse, I became intensely imbued with personal interest in what was going on. I seemed to feel that I had an important part to play, without exactly understanding what it was. Against the crowd which environed me, however, I experienced a deep sentiment of animosity. I shrank from amid them, and, swiftly, by a circuitous path, reached and entered the city. Here all was the wildest tumult and contention. A small party of men, clad in garments half Indian, half European, and officered by gentlemen in a uniform partly British, were engaged, at great odds, with the swarming rabble of the allies. I joined the weaker party, arming myself with the weapons of a fallen officer, and fighting I knew not whom with the nervous ferocity of despair. We were soon overpowered by numbers, and driven to seek refuge in a species of kiosk. Here we barricaded ourselves, and, for the present, were secure. From a loop-hole near the summit of the kiosk, I perceived a vast crowd, in furious agitation, surrounding and assaulting a gay palace that overhung the river. Presently,

from an upper window of this palace, there descended an effemi-
nate-looking person, by means of a string made of the turbans of
his attendants. A boat was at hand in which he escaped to the
opposite bank of the river.

'And now a new object took possession of my soul. I spoke a
few hurried but energetic words to my companions, and, having
succeeded in gaining over a few of them to my purpose, made a
frantic sally from the kiosk. We rushed amid the crowd that
surrounded it. They retreated, at first, before us. They rallied,
fought madly, and retreated again. In the meantime we were
borne far from the kiosk, and became bewildered and entangled
among the narrow streets of tall, overhanging houses, into the
recess of which the sun had never been able to shine. The rabble
pressed impetuously upon us, harassing us with their spears, and
overwhelming us with flights of arrows. These latter were very
remarkable, and resembled in some respects the writhing creese of
the Malay. They were made to imitate the body of a creeping
serpent, and were long and black, with a poisoned barb. One of
them struck me upon the right temple. I reeled and fell. An
instantaneous and dreadful sickness seized me. I struggled—I
gasped—I died.'

'You will hardly persist *now*,' said I, smiling, 'that the whole of
your adventure was not a dream. You are not prepared to maintain that you are dead?'

When I said these words, I of course expected some lively sally
from Bedloe in reply; but, to my astonishment, he hesitated,
trembled, became fearfully pallid, and remained silent. I looked
toward Templeton. He sat erect and rigid in his chair—his teeth
chattered, and his eyes were starting from their sockets. 'Proceed!'
he at length said hoarsely to Bedloe.

'For many minutes,' continued the latter, 'my sole sentiment—
my sole feeling—was that of darkness and nonentity, with the
consciousness of death. At length there seemed to pass a violent
and sudden shock through my soul, as if of electricity. With it
came the sense of elasticity and of light. This latter I felt—not saw.
In an instant I seemed to rise from the ground. But I had no bodily,
no visible, audible, or palpable presence. The crowd had departed. The tumult had ceased. The city was in comparative
repose. Beneath me lay my corpse, with the arrow in my temple,
the whole head greatly swollen and disfigured. But all these things
I felt—not saw. I took interest in nothing. Even the corpse seemed a
matter in which I had no concern. Volition I had none, but

appeared to be impelled into motion, and flitted buoyantly out of the city, retracing the circuitous path by which I had entered it. When I had attained that point of the ravine in the mountains at which I had encountered the hyena, I again experienced a shock as of a galvanic battery; the sense of weight, of volition, of substance, returned. I became my original self, and bent my steps eagerly homeward—but the past had not lost the vividness of the real—and not now, even for an instant, can I compel my understanding to regard it as a dream.'

'Nor was it,' said Templeton, with an air of deep solemnity, 'yet it would be difficult to say how otherwise it should be termed. Let us suppose only, that the soul of the man of to-day is upon the verge of some stupendous psychal discoveries. Let us content ourselves with this supposition. For the rest I have some explanation to make. Here is a water-colour drawing, which I should have shown you before, but which an accountable sentiment of horror has hitherto prevented me from showing.'

We looked at the picture which he presented. I saw nothing in it of an extraordinary character; but its effect upon Bedloe was prodigious. He nearly fainted as he gazed. And yet it was but a miniature portrait—a miraculously accurate one, to be sure—of his own very remarkable features. At least this was my thought as I regarded it.

'You will perceive,' said Templeton, 'the date of this picture—it is here, scarcely visible, in this corner—1780. In this year was the portrait taken. It is the likeness of a dead friend—a Mr Oldeb—to whom I became much attached at Calcutta, during the administration of Warren Hastings. I was then only twenty years old. When I first saw you, Mr Bedloe, at Saratoga, it was the miraculous similarity which existed between yourself and the painting which induced me to accost you, to seek your friendship, and to bring about those arrangements which resulted in my becoming your constant companion. In accomplishing this point, I was urged partly, and perhaps principally, by a regretful memory of the deceased, but also, in part, by an uneasy, and not altogether horrorless curiosity respecting yourself.

'In your detail of the vision which presented itself to you amid the hills, you have described, with the minutest accuracy, the Indian city of Benares, upon the Holy River. The riots, the combat, the massacre, were the actual events of the insurrection of Cheyte Sing, which took place in 1780, when Hastings was put in imminent peril of his life. The man escaping by the string of turbans was Cheyte Sing himself. The party in the kiosk were sepoys and British officers, headed by Hastings. Of this party I was one, and did all I could to prevent the rash and fatal sally of the officer who fell, in the crowded alleys, by the poisoned arrow of a Bengalee. That officer was my dearest friend. It was Oldeb. You will perceive by these manuscripts' (here the speaker produced a note-book in which several pages appeared to have been freshly written), 'that at the very period in which you fancied these things amid the hills I was engaged in detailing them upon paper here at home.'

In about a week after this conversation, the following paragraphs appeared in a Charlottesville paper:

'We have the painful duty of announcing the death of Mr AUGUSTUS BEDLO, a gentleman whose amiable manners and many virtues have long endeared him to the citizens of Charlottesville.

'Mr B., for some years past, has been subject to neuralgia, which has often threatened to terminate fatally; but this can be regarded only as the mediate cause of his decease. The proximate cause was one of especial singularity. In an excursion to the Ragged Mountains, a few days since, a slight cold and fever were contracted, attended with great determination of blood to the head. To relieve this, Dr Templeton resorted to topical bleeding. Leeches were applied to the temples. In a fearfully brief period the patient died, when it appeared that, in the jar containing the leeches, had been introduced, by accident, one of the venomous vermicular sangsues which are now and then found in the neighbouring ponds. This creature fastened itself upon a small artery in the right temple. Its close resemblance to the medical leech caused the mistake to be overlooked until too late.

'N.B.—The poisonous sangsue of Charlottesville may always be distinguished from the medicinal leech by its blackness, and especially by its writhing or vermicular motions, which very nearly resemble those of a snake.'

I was speaking with the editor of the paper in question, upon the topic of this remarkable accident, when it occurred to me to ask how it happened that the name of the deceased had been given as Bedlo.

'I presume,' said I, 'you have authority for this spelling, but I have always supposed the name to be written with an *e* at the end.'

'Authority?—no,' he replied. 'It is a mere typographical error. The name is Bedlo with an *e*, all the world over, and I never knew it to be spelt otherwise in my life.'

'Then,' said I mutteringly, as I turned upon my heel, 'then indeed has it come to pass that one truth is stranger than any fiction—for Bedlo, without the *e*, what is it but Oldeb conversed? And this man tells me it is a typographical error.'

Ray Bradbury

A Sound of Thunder

The sign on the wall seemed to quaver under a film of sliding warm water. Eckels felt his eyelids blink over his stare, and the sign burned in this momentary darkness:

> TIME SAFARI, INC.
> SAFARIS TO ANY YEAR IN THE PAST.
> YOU NAME THE ANIMAL.
> WE TAKE YOU THERE.
> YOU SHOOT IT.

A warm phlegm gathered in Eckels' throat; he swallowed and pushed it down. The muscles around his mouth formed a smile as he put his hand slowly out upon the air, and in that hand waved a check for ten thousand dollars to the man behind the desk.

'Does this safari guarantee I come back alive?'

'We guarantee nothing,' said the official, 'except the dinosaurs.' He turned. 'This is Mr Travis, your Safari Guide in the Past. He'll tell you what and where to shoot. If he says no shooting, no shooting. If you disobey instructions, there's a stiff penalty of another ten thousand dollars, plus possible government action, on your return.'

Eckels glanced across the vast office at a mass and tangle, a snaking and humming of wires and steel boxes, at an aurora that flickered now orange, now silver, now blue. There was a sound like a gigantic bonfire burning all of Time, all the years and all the parchment calendars, all the hours piled high and set aflame.

A touch of the hand and this burning would, on the instant, beautifully reverse itself. Eckels remembered the wording in the advertisements to the letter. Out of chars and ashes, out of dust and coals, like golden salamanders, the old years, the green years, might leap; roses sweeten the air, white hair turn Irish-black, wrinkles vanish; all, everything fly back to seed, flee death, rush down to their beginnings, suns rise in western skies and set in glorious easts, moons eat themselves opposite to the custom, all and everything cupping one in another like Chinese boxes, rabbits in hats, all and everything returning to the fresh death, the seed death, the green death, to the time before the beginning. A touch of a hand might do it, the merest touch of a hand.

'Hell and damn,' Eckels breathed, the light of the Machine on his thin face. 'A real Time Machine.' He shook his head. 'Makes you think. If the election had gone badly yesterday, I might be here now running away from the results. Thank God Keith won. He'll make a fine President of the United States.'

'Yes,' said the man behind the desk. 'We're lucky. If Deutscher had gotten in, we'd have the worst kind of dictatorship. There's an anti-everything man for you, a militarist, anti-Christ, anti-human, anti-intellectual. People called us up, you know, joking but not joking. Said if Deutscher became President they wanted to go live in 1492. Of course it's not our business to conduct Escapes, but to form Safaris. Anyway, Keith's President now. All you got to worry about is—'

'Shooting my dinosaur,' Eckels finished it for him.

'*A Tyrannosaurus rex*. The Thunder Lizard, the damnedest monster in history. Sign this release. Anything happens to you, we're not responsible. Those dinosaurs are hungry.'

Eckels flushed angrily. 'Trying to scare me!'

'Frankly, yes. We don't want anyone going who'll panic at the first shot. Six Safari leaders were killed last year, and a dozen hunters. We're here to give you the damnedest thrill a *real* hunter ever asked for. Travelling you back sixty million years to bag the biggest damned game in all Time. Your personal cheque's still there. Tear it up.'

Mr Eckels looked at the cheque for a long time. His fingers twitched.

'Good luck,' said the man behind the desk. 'Mr Travis, he's all yours.'

They moved silently across the room, taking their guns with them, toward the Machine, toward the silver metal and the roaring light.

First a day and then a night and then a day and then a night, then it was day-night-day-night-day. A week, a month, a year, a decade! A.D. 2055. A.D. 2019. 1999! 1957! Gone! The Machine roared.

They put on their oxygen helmets and tested the intercoms.

Eckels swayed on the padded seat, his face pale, his jaw stiff. He felt the trembling in his arms and he looked down and found his hands tight on the new rifle. There were four other men in the Machine. Travis, the Safari Leader, his assistant, Lesperance, and two other hunters, Billings and Kramer. They sat looking at each other, and the years blazed around them.

'Can these guns get a dinosaur cold?' Eckels felt his mouth saying.

'If you hit them right,' said Travis on the helmet radio. 'Some dinosaurs have two brains, one in the head, another far down the spinal column. We stay away from those. That's stretching luck. Put your first two shots into the eyes, if you can, blind them, and go back into the brain.'

The Machine howled. Time was a film run backward. Suns fled and ten million moons fled after them. 'Good God,' said Eckels. 'Every hunter that ever lived would envy us today. This makes Africa seem like Illinois.'

The Machine slowed; its scream fell to a murmur. The Machine stopped.

The sun stopped in the sky.

The fog that had enveloped the Machine blew away and they were in an old time, a very old time indeed, three hunters and two Safari Heads with their blue metal guns across their knees.

'Christ isn't born yet,' said Travis. 'Moses has not gone to the mountain to talk with God. The Pyramids are still in the earth, waiting to be cut out and put up. *Remember* that, Alexander, Caesar, Napoleon, Hitler—none of them exists.'

The men nodded.

'That'—Mr Travis pointed—'is the jungle of sixty million two thousand and fifty-five years before President Keith.'

He indicated a metal path that struck off into green wilderness, over steaming swamp, among giant ferns and palms.

'And that,' he said, 'is the Path, laid by Time Safari for your use. It floats six inches above the earth. Doesn't touch so much as one grass blade, flower, or tree. It's an antigravity metal. Its purpose is to keep you from touching this world of the past in any way. Stay on the Path. Don't go off it. I repeat. *Don't go off.* For *any* reason! If you fall off, there's a penalty. And don't shoot any animal we don't okay.'

'Why?' asked Eckels.

They sat in the ancient wilderness. Far birds' cries blew on a wind, and the smell of tar and an old salt sea, moist grasses, and flowers the colour of blood.

'We don't want to change the Future. We don't belong here in the Past. The government doesn't *like* us here. We have to pay big graft to keep our franchise. A Time Machine is damn finicky business. Not knowing it, we might kill an important animal, a small bird, a roach, a flower even, thus destroying an important link in a growing species.'

'That's not clear,' said Eckels.

'All right,' Travis continued, 'say we accidentally kill one mouse here. That means all the future families of this one particular mouse are destroyed, right?'

'Right.'

'And all the families of the families of that one mouse! With a stamp of your foot, you annihilate first one, then a dozen, then a thousand, a million, a *billion* possible mice!'

'So they're dead,' said Eckels. 'So what?'

'So what?' Travis snorted quietly. 'Well, what about the foxes that'll need those mice to survive? For want of ten mice, a fox dies. For want of ten foxes, a lion starves. For want of a lion, all manner of insects, vultures, infinite billions of life forms are thrown into chaos and destruction. Eventually it all boils down to this: fifty-nine million years later, a cave man, one of a dozen on the *entire* world, goes hunting wild boar or sabre-tooth tiger for food. But you, friend, have *stepped* on all the tigers in that region. By stepping on *one* single mouse. So the cave man starves. And the cave man, please note, is not just *any* expendable man, no! He is an *entire future nation*. From his loins would have sprung ten sons. From *their* loins one hundred sons, and thus onward to a civilization. Destroy this one man, and you destroy a race, a people, an entire history of life. It is comparable to slaying some of Adam's grandchildren. The stomp of your foot, on one mouse, could start an earthquake, the effects of which could shake our earth and destinies down through Time, to their very foundations. With the death of that one cave man, a billion others yet unborn are throttled in the womb. Perhaps Rome never rises on its seven hills. Perhaps Europe is forever a dark forest, and only Asia waxes healthy and teeming. Step on a mouse and you crush the Pyramids. Step on a mouse and you leave your print, like a Grand Canyon, across Eternity. Queen Elizabeth might never be born, Washington might not cross the Delaware, there might never be a United States at all. So be careful. Stay on the Path. *Never* step off!'

'I see,' said Eckels. 'Then it wouldn't pay for us even to touch the *grass*?'

'Correct. Crushing certain plants could add up infinitesimally. A little error here would multiply in sixty million years, all out of proportion. Of course maybe our theory is wrong. Maybe Time *can't* be changed by us. Or maybe it can be changed only in little subtle ways. A dead mouse here makes an insect imbalance there, a population disproportion later, a bad harvest further on, a depression, mass starvation, and, finally, a change in *social* temperament in far-flung countries. Something much more subtle, like that. Perhaps only a soft breath, a whisper, a hair, pollen on the air, such a slight, slight change that unless you looked close you wouldn't see it. Who knows? Who really can say he knows? We don't know. We're guessing. But until we do know for certain whether our messing around in Time *can* make a big roar or a little rustle in history, we're being damned careful. This Machine, this Path, your clothing and bodies, were sterilized, as you know, before the journey. We wear these oxygen helmets so we can't introduce our bacteria into an ancient atmosphere.'

'How do we know which animals to shoot?'

'They're marked with red paint,' said Travis. 'Today, before our journey, we sent Lesperance here back with the Machine. He came to this particular era and followed certain animals.'

'Studying them?'

'Right,' said Lesperance. 'I track them through their entire existence, noting which of them lives longest. Very few. How many times they mate. Not often. Life's short. When I find one that's going to die when a tree falls on him, or one that drowns in a tar pit, I note the exact hour, minute, and second. I shoot a paint bomb. It leaves a red patch on his hide. We can't miss it. Then I correlate our arrival in the Past so that we meet the Monster not more than two minutes before he would have died anyway. This way, we kill only animals with no future, that are never going to mate again. You see how *careful* we are?'

'But if you came back this morning in Time,' said Eckels eagerly, 'you must've bumped into *us*, our Safari! How did it turn out? Was it successful? Did all of us get through—alive?'

Travis and Lesperance gave each other a look.

'That'd be a paradox,' said the latter. 'Time doesn't permit that sort of mess—a man meeting himself. When such occasions threaten. Time steps aside. Like an airplane hitting an air pocket. You felt the Machine jump just before we stopped? That was us passing ourselves on the way back to the Future. We saw nothing. There's no way of telling *if* this expedition was a success, *if* we got our monster, or whether all of—meaning *you*, Mr Eckels—got out alive.'

Eckels smiled palely.

'Cut that,' said Travis sharply. 'Everyone on his feet!'

They were ready to leave the Machine.

The jungle was high and the jungle was broad and the jungle was the entire world forever and forever. Sounds like music and sounds like flying tents filled the sky, and those were pterodactyls soaring with cavernous grey wings, gigantic bats out of a delirium and a night fever. Eckles, balanced on the narrow Path, aimed his rifle playfully.

'Stop that!' said Travis. 'Don't even aim for fun, damn it! If your gun should go off—'

Eckels blushed. 'Where's our *Tyrannosaurus?*'

Lesperance checked his wrist watch. 'Up ahead. We'll bisect his trail in sixty seconds. Look for the red paint, for Christ's sake. Don't shoot till we give the word. Stay on the Path. *Stay on the Path!*'

They moved forward in the wind of morning.

'Strange,' murmured Eckels. 'Up ahead, sixty million years, Election Day over. Keith made President. Everyone celebrating. And here we are, a million years lost, and they don't exist. The things we worried about for months, a lifetime, not even born or thought about yet.'

'Safety catches off, everyone!' ordered Travis. 'You, first shot, Eckles. Second, Billings, Third, Kramer.'

'I've hunted tiger, wild boar, buffalo, elephant, but Jesus, this is *it*,' said Eckels. 'I'm shaking like a kid.'

'Ah,' said Travis.

Everyone stopped.

Travis raised his hand. 'Ahead,' he whispered. 'In the mist. There he is. There's His Royal Majesty now.'

The jungle was wide and full of twitterings, rustlings, murmurs, and sighs.

Suddenly it all ceased, as if someone had shut a door.

Silence.

A sound of thunder.

Out of the mist, one hundred yards away, came *Tyrannosaurus rex*.

'Jesus God,' whispered Eckels.

'Sh!'

It came on great oiled, resilient, striding legs. It towered thirty feet above half of the trees, a great evil god, folding its delicate watchmaker's claws close to its oily reptilian chest. Each lower leg was a piston, a thousand pounds of white bone, sunk in thick ropes of muscle, sheathed over in a gleam of pebbled skin like the mail of a terrible warrior. Each thigh was a ton of meat, ivory, and steel mesh. And from the great breathing cage of the upper body those two delicate arms dangled out front, arms with hands which might pick up and examine men like toys, while the snake neck coiled. And the head itself, a ton of sculptured stone, lifted easily upon the sky. Its mouth gaped, exposing a fence of teeth like daggers. Its eyes rolled, ostrich eggs, empty of all expression save hunger. It closed its mouth in a death grin. It ran, its pelvic bones crushing aside trees and bushes, its taloned feet clawing damp earth, leaving prints six inches deep wherever it settled its weight. It ran with a gliding ballet step, far too poised and balanced for its ten tons. It moved into a sunlit arena warily, its beautifully reptile hands feeling the air.

'My God!' Eckels twitched his mouth. 'It could reach up and grab the moon.'

'Sh!' Travis jerked angrily. 'He hasn't seen us yet.'

'It can't be killed.' Eckels pronounced this verdict quietly, as if there could be no argument. He had weighed the evidence and this was his considered opinion. The rifle in his hands seemed a cap gun. 'We were fools to come. This is impossible.'

'Shut up!' hissed Travis.

'Nightmare.'

'Turn around,' commanded Travis. 'Walk quietly to the Machine. We'll remit one-half your fee.'

'I didn't realize it would be this *big*,' said Eckels. 'I miscalculated, that's all. And now I want out.'

'It sees us!'

'There's the red paint on its chest!'

The Thunder Lizard raised itself. Its armoured flesh glittered like a thousand green coins. The coins, crusted with slime, steamed. In the slime, tiny insects wriggled, so that the entire body seemed to twitch and undulate, even while the monster itself did not move. It exhaled. The stink of raw flesh blew down the wilderness.

'Get me out of here,' said Eckels. 'It was never like this before. I was always sure I'd come through alive. I had good guides, good safaris, and safety. This time, I figured wrong. I've met my match and admit it. This is too much for me to get hold of.'

'Don't run,' said Lesperance. 'Turn around. Hide in the Machine.'

'Yes.' Eckels seemed to be numb. He looked at his feet as if trying to make them move. He gave a grunt of helplessness.

'Eckels!'

He took a few steps, blinking, shuffling.

'Not *that* way!'

The Monster, at the first motion, lunged forward with a terrible scream. It covered one hundred yards in four seconds. The rifles jerked up and blazed fire. A windstorm from the beast's mouth engulfed them in the stench of slime and old blood. The Monster roared, teeth glittering with sun.

Eckels, not looking back, walked blindly to the edge of the Path, his gun limp in his arms, stepped off the Path, and walked, not knowing it, in the jungle. His feet sank into green moss. His legs moved him, and he felt alone and remote from the events behind.

The rifles cracked again. Their sound was lost in shriek and lizard thunder. The great lever of the reptile's tail swung up, lashed sideways. Trees exploded in clouds of leaf and branch. The Monster twitched its jeweller's hands down to fondle at the men, to twist them in half, to crush them like berries, to cram them into its teeth and its screaming throat. Its boulder-stone eyes levelled with the men. They saw themselves mirrored. They fired at the metallic eyelids and the blazing black iris.

Like a stone idol, like a mountain avalanche, *Tyrannosaurus* fell. Thundering, it clutched trees, pulled them with it. It wrenched and tore the metal Path. The men flung themselves back and away. The body hit, ten tons of cold flesh and stone. The guns fired. The Monster lashed its armoured tail, twitched its snake jaws, and lay still. A fount of blood spurted from its throat. Somewhere inside, a sac of fluids burst. Sickening gushes drenched the hunters. They stood, red and glistening.

The thunder faded.

The jungle was silent. After the avalanche, a green peace. After the nightmare, nothing.

Billings and Kramer sat on the pathway and threw up. Travis and Lesperance stood with smoking rifles, cursing steadily.

In the Time Machine, on his face, Eckels lay shivering.

He had found his way back to the Path, climbed into the Machine.

Travis came walking, glanced at Eckels, took cotton gauze from a metal box, and returned to the others, who were sitting on the Path.

'Clean up.'

They wiped the blood from their helmets. They began to curse too. The Monster lay, a hill of solid flesh. Within, you could hear the sighs and murmurs as the furthest chambers of it died, the organs malfunctioning, liquids running a final instant from pocket to sac to spleen, everything shutting off, closing up forever. It was like standing by a wrecked locomotive or a steam shovel at quitting time, all valves being released or levered tight. Bones cracked; the tonnage of its own flesh, off balance, dead weight, snapped the delicate forearms, caught underneath. The meat settled, quivering.

Another cracking sound. Overhead, a gigantic tree branch broke from its heavy mooring, fell. It crashed upon the dead beast with finality.

'There.' Lesperance checked his watch. 'Right on time. That's the giant tree that was scheduled to fall and kill this animal originally.' He glanced at the two hunters. 'You want the trophy picture?'

'What?'

'We can't take a trophy back to the Future. The body has to stay right here where it would have died originally, so the insects, birds, and bacteria can get at it, as they were intended to. Everything in balance. The body stays. But we *can* take a picture of you standing near it.'

The two men tried to think, but gave up, shaking their heads.

They let themselves be led along the metal Path. They sank wearily into the Machine cushions. They gazed back at the ruined Monster, the stagnating mound, where already strange reptilian birds and golden insects were busy at the steaming armour.

A sound on the floor of the Time Machine stiffened them. Eckels sat there, shivering.

'I'm sorry,' he said at last.

'Get up!' cried Travis.

Eckels got up.

'Go out on that Path alone,' said Travis. He had his rifle pointed. 'You're not coming back in the Machine. We're leaving you here!'

Lesperance seized Travis' arm. 'Wait—'

'Stay out of this!' Travis shook his hand away. 'This son of a bitch nearly killed us. But it isn't *that* so much. Hell, no. It's his *shoes!* Look at them! He ran off the Path. My God, that *ruins* us! Christ knows how much we'll forfeit. Tens of thousands of dollars of insurance! We guarantee no one leaves the Path. He left it. Oh, the damn fool! I'll have to report to the government. They might revoke our licence to travel. God knows *what* he's done to Time, to History!'

'Take it easy, all he did was kick up some dirt.'

'How do we *know?*' cried Travis. 'We don't know anything! It's all a damn mystery! Get out there, Eckels!'

Eckels fumbled his shirt. 'I'll pay anything. A hundred thousand dollars!'

Travis glared at Eckels' chequebook and spat. 'Go out there. The Monster's next to the Path. Stick your arms up to your elbows in his mouth. Then you can come back with us.'

'That's unreasonable!'

'The Monster's dead, you yellow bastard. The bullets! The bullets can't be left behind. They don't belong in the Past; they might change something. Here's my knife. Dig them out!'

The jungle was alive again, full of the old tremorings and bird cries. Eckels turned slowly to regard the primeval garbage dump, that hill of nightmares and terror. After a long time, like a sleep-walker, he shuffled out along the Path.

He returned, shuddering, five minutes later, his arms soaked and red to the elbows. He held out his hands. Each held a number of steel bullets. Then he fell. He lay where he fell, not moving.

'You didn't have to make him do that,' said Lesperance.

'Didn't I? It's too early to tell.' Travis nudged the still body. 'He'll live. Next time he won't go hunting game like this. Okay.' He jerked his thumb wearily at Lesperance. 'Switch on. Let's go home.'

1492. 1776. 1812.

They cleaned their hands and faces. They changed their caking shirts and pants. Eckels was up and around again, not speaking. Travis glared at him for a full ten minutes.

'Don't look at me,' cried Eckels. 'I haven't done anything.'

'Who can tell?'

'Just ran off the Path, that's all, a little mud on my shoes—what do you want me to do—get down and pray?'

'We might need it. I'm warning you, Eckels, I might kill you yet. I've got my gun ready.'

'I'm innocent. I've done nothing!'

1999. 2000. 2055.

The Machine stopped.

'Get out,' said Travis.

The room was there as they had left it. But not the same as they had left it. The same man sat behind the same desk. But the same man did not quite sit behind the same desk.

Travis looked around swiftly. 'Everything okay here?' he snapped.

'Fine. Welcome home!'

Travis did not relax. He seemed to be looking at the very atoms of the air itself, at the way the sun poured through the one high window.

'Okay, Eckels, get out. Don't ever come back.'

Eckels could not move.

'You heard me,' said Travis. 'What're you *staring* at?'

Eckels stood smelling of the air, and there was a thing to the air, a chemical taint so subtle, so slight, that only a faint cry of his subliminal senses warned him it was there. The colours, white, grey, blue, orange, in the wall, in the furniture, in the sky beyond the window, were . . . were . . . And there was a *feel*. His flesh twitched. His hands twitched. He stood drinking the oddness with the pores of his body. Somewhere, someone must have been screaming one of those whistles that only a dog can hear. His body screamed silence in return. Beyond this room, beyond this wall, beyond this man who was not quite the same man seated at this desk that was not quite the same desk . . . lay an entire world of streets and people. What sort of world it was now, there was no telling. He could feel them moving there, beyond the walls, almost, like so many chess pieces blown in a dry wind . . .

But the immediate thing was the sign painted on the office wall, the same sign he had read earlier today on first entering.

Somehow, the sign had changed:

> TYME SEFARI INC.
> SEFARIS TU ANY YEER EN THE PAST.
> YU NAIM THE ANIMALL.
> WEE TAEK YOU THAIR.
> YU SHOOT ITT.

Eckels felt himself fall into a chair. He fumbled crazily at the thick slime on his boots. He held up a clod of dirt, trembling. 'No, it *can't* be. Not a *little* thing like that. No!'

Embedded in the mud, glistening green and gold and black, was a butterfly, very beautiful, and very dead.

'Not a little thing like *that!* Not a butterfly!' cried Eckels.

It fell to the floor, an exquisite thing, a small thing that could upset balances and knock down a line of small dominoes and then big dominoes and then gigantic dominoes, all down the years across Time. Eckels' mind whirled. It *couldn't* change things. Killing one butterfly couldn't be *that* important! Could it?

His face was cold. His mouth trembled, asking: 'Who—who won the presidential election yesterday?'

The man behind the desk laughed. 'You joking? You know damn well. Deutscher, of course! Who else? Not that damn weakling Keith. We got an iron man now, a man with guts, by God!' The official stopped. 'What's wrong?'

Eckels moaned. He dropped to his knees. He scrabbled at the golden butterfly with shaking fingers. 'Can't we,' he pleaded to the world, to himself, to the officials, to the Machine, 'can't we take it *back*, can't we *make* it alive again? Can't we start over? Can't we—'

He did not move. Eyes shut, he waited, shivering. He heard Travis breathe loud in the room; he heard Travis shift his rifle, click the safety catch, and raise the weapon.

There was a sound of thunder.

The Edwin Tree

I am at something of a loss how to begin. I have, you see, in my travels about this county, in my researches into the strange traditions and tales of the Peak District, heard of many inexplicable, odd, and sometimes disquieting phenomena, but always what I heard came second-hand, from another's mouth, so it was easy enough to shrug one's shoulders and say to oneself: 'These things may be believed by simple country folk, but I am a man of the Nineteenth Century, a man of science, I am not taken in by such things. There are explanations, reasons . . .'

However, in the case of the story of the Edwin tree, I saw these things with my own eyes, and ever since have turned them over in my mind, searching for some rational explanation, to tie it all up neatly somehow so that I could present it to the reader as simply a *tale*. But there seems to be no way of tying it up neatly. The things that I saw and heard reverberate, vibrate in my mind, returning again and again to vex and puzzle me. So I can tell it to you as I saw and heard it, and try to be as clear and honest as it is in my power to be.

I will begin on that morning in December, when I found myself on the moors, making my way to the village of B . . . . I had risen early, put on my warmest walking clothes and my stoutest boots and, with compass, map and notebook, considered myself well equipped for a day's research.

The sky was cloudless, and the air, though keen, had a refreshing bite to it. It soon grew warm under my layers of clothing. There was, to be sure, a cold wind which stung my cheeks and made my eyes water, but by the time B . . . was in sight I was enjoying myself too much to notice that.

I stopped for a moment for a warming draught from my brandy-flask, to take in the stark beauty of the scene, and to consult my map for a way down to the village.

As I turned my head I noticed, some way behind me, coming along the track which I had just walked over, a figure following.

He was too far away to be clearly made out, but near enough for me to see that he was pulling behind him some kind of handcart, of the kind peddlars or tinkers use.

I decided to wait for him. It would be pleasant to have some company for a while. And I was, I must confess, intrigued to know what was in the curious cart that he was dragging along behind him.

So it happened, that as soon as he could be supposed to be within earshot, I called out to him:

'Hello! Hello there!'

When he heard my voice, he stopped, raised his head and searched around. I called again.

'Hello! Over here!'

He swung his head slowly from side to side, searching. Then he saw me. He began again to walk with an odd, lurching gait which his cart, in its way, imitated. Soon he was close enough to be made out more clearly.

How shall I describe him to you? He has so often haunted my dreams since that I find it difficult to cast my mind back to my first impression.

He was dressed in black, from head to toe in black, rather like an out-of-work undertaker, slightly shabby but keeping up appearances, yes, there was more than a whiff of the cemetery about him. He wore a wide-brimmed but somewhat ill-used hat, a black suit stained by mud and rain and stout, though very battered boots. His face was, I could now see, hidden by the brim of his hat, for pulling his cart he peered at the uneven stony track he passed along. But in a matter of moments he had come up almost to where I was. He stopped. He allowed the shafts of his cart to fall from his hands. He straightened up and looked me in the eye.

'God be with ye, sir,' he said.

I looked into the face of this man. A remarkable face. His cheeks were sunken and as pale and wasted as bone. Thin eyebrows surmounted eyes of a startling blue which fixed themselves on mine in a way which made me feel suddenly cold, and a little frightened of him. He was very tall, and of an alarming bony thinness, as if he had been very ill, perhaps near to death.

'Where are you heading, friend?' I asked him.

'To B . . . , God willing. And you?'

'The same.'

'Praise the Lord, I have been sent for.'

Not knowing what to make of this last remark. 'Then perhaps we may journey together,' I suggested, 'I would welcome your company.'

'So be it, then,' the man said. 'My name is Heathcote. Gregory Heathcote.'

'And mine is Wood. William Wood.'

We shook hands. It was an extremely chilly handshake. Then, without another word my new friend bent himself before his cart and we moved down the track.

He spoke hardly a word. His silence and the inward dark intentness of his movements stopped my own mouth and made me shy of him, and unwilling to open a conversation. He was indeed a morose and depressing companion. I began to regret calling to him. I wondered in my mind about the man, and the contents of that cart, which continued to intrigue me. Could he be a priest? There was indeed a clerical cut about his dress. As to his cart, it was covered with a tarpaulin and I could only guess at what it might contain. Soon curiosity gained the upper hand. I swallowed my fear and asked him directly.

'My cart, sir? It contains weapons, sir.'

'Weapons?'

'Aye, sir. Weapons of the Lord. I have been sent for.'

My curiosity was now thoroughly aroused. However I guessed from his manner that he did not wish to be pressed further, and we walked the rest of the way in silence.

The village of B . . . , which I had never visited before, proved to be a pleasant, secluded little place. The dwellings for the most part stand on the slope of a steep hill. At the base of the hut-crowded ridge stand some more substantial buildings: the church and the inn.

As we came into the village itself, Heathcote stopped.

'Thank you for your society, sir. I will leave you now.'

'Well . . . thank you for yours,' I replied.

He turned his back on me, and tugging the cart behind him, made off down the village street. I watched him till he disappeared from view around a corner. I must confess that I was not sorry to be rid of his gloomy presence, though now that I was alone I was at a loss to know what to do next.

I had come to B . . . to find tales and fancies from the local folk, I had my notebook in my pocket, but, for some reason my desire to pursue such things had left me. Perhaps it was because I sensed that my travelling companion, the oddly intent Heathcote, was here on much graver, weightier business than my own. However, the walk had given me an appetite, and I decided to make for the inn. The place was warm and there was a roaring log fire. I secured a place beside it, and with a plate of the landlord's excellent soup and a cob of bread before me began to feel much warmer.

I have heard many interesting tales in establishments of this kind, and have often been drawn in by overhearing the general talk for a few moments. In just this manner I observed two men at a nearby table talking to the landlady of the inn, their heads close together as if they were discussing important matters. I will try to reproduce their conversation for you, as accurately as memory may allow.

'I've heard it's today he's coming,' said the woman, 'he were seen . . .'

'Aye, happen it's today,' said one man.

'He's been seen, tha knows,' said the other.

'Poor lass, poor lass,' and here the woman lowered her voice, so that I could hardly make out her words, and seemed to be on the verge of tears.

One man placed a comforting hand upon her shoulder.

'She's gone now, Betty love . . .' he said softly.

'Gone perhaps,' the woman Betty cried, 'but not at rest!'

'Aye, we know that, Betty,' said her friend, 'but we shouldn't talk about them things!'

'I hope he can do summat, that I do,' said Betty.

'They say he's a clever feller,' said one of her companions. 'He knows herbs and the planets and stars, and he's a fine preacher they say. A man of God.'

'T'vicar's a man of God,' Betty said. 'And he doesn't want nowt to do wi 'im.'

'Gar, the vicar's old-fashioned. He tried, didn't he, and couldn't do owt.'

'That's why he don't like Heathcote,' said the other man. 'He's jealous if tha asks me. The vicar's just for praying an' that. They say Heathcote's got summat: stronger than prayin'.'

I suspect that you can well imagine my feelings at hearing Heathcote's name. I was on the point of breaking into their talk, when the door of the inn flew open and in dashed a youth, hair flying and pale face contorted with excitement.

'He's h-h-h-here! M—h-he's here!' he stammered breathlessly.

'Where, Adam, where?' asked the landlady, her face alive with expectation.

'At t'Edwin tree! Folks is coming out of their houses! They're all going down to the tree to h-h-h-hear him!—Everybody's going! Th-th-tha s'l have ter hurry! It's beginnin'!'

In a matter of moments, the inn was empty. What could I do but follow on?

I had heard of this Edwin tree. It seems that after a battle in the neighbourhood, the defeated King Edwin had been taken by his enemies and hanged from one of its boughs. Beyond this fact, I knew little. But to this tree, I, and it seemed all of the inhabitants of B . . . beside, were now making our way. We passed through the village, beyond the market square and the church, and into a field where grew, sure enough, a fine old oak, bare-branched now, sturdy and impressive. Around it, a gathering circle of villagers, waiting. Some sat on the ground, some stood. It might have been a village picnic, but for two things: there were no children there, and the faces of the people, which were serious and set, fitter for a funeral than any kind of celebration.

I edged my way forward through the crowd. On the grass before the great oak had been spread a purple cloth; about four yards square; and set on the cloth at intervals of about a foot, a circle of lighted candles set inside bottles, against the wind. Some of the contents, perhaps, of Heathcote's . . .

I speculated no further, for at that moment, like an actor walking on to a stage, Heathcote himself came out from behind a tree. The crowd fell silent. He swept them with his eyes, for the slightest moment catching mine and looking straight *at* me. I felt at once the coldness of the man.

'Will someone tell me what has happened here?' he commanded.

One person turned to the next and heads craned round to see who would speak. For a moment it seemed that none would. Then . . .

'I will. I'll tell.'

It was the woman from the inn, the landlady. She stepped forward two steps, into the ring.

'The Lord has prompted thee, woman,' intoned Heathcote. 'Speak, then.'

'She were murdered, sir, the little lass, under this very tree. Nobody can say who did it. They found her buried under the tree with her little throat cut. She were only five year old, then, when it happened, two years since. Joe and Annie, them's her parents, grieved so, poor souls, that they moved away to Chesterfield. They were friends to me . . .'

And the poor woman began to weep.

'Come, my child,' Heathcote said, placing a skeletal hand upon her shoulder. 'Why was I sent for?'

'She's still here! Still here, sir, that's why we sent. Her poor soul moves about the tree like a shadow. We hear her voice on the wind, weeping and carrying on so, not a soul in the village can sleep at night for it. They'll tell thee!'

And she swept her arm round the circle to include them all. Afraid, they shrank from her.

'Poor little one,' the woman continued, weeping. 'Poor little one! She has no peace or rest! And we have none either, for hearing her!'

'And when did this visitation begin?'

'A year ago, sir, the same night as when it . . . happened.'

'Why,' Heathcote asked in a booming voice, 'was I not sent for sooner?'

The crowd drew back from him shamefaced, like guilty children. But one man stayed where he was to answer him.

'I'll tell thee why, sir! It were t'vicar. He came here, wi' bell and book and candle, and said prayers an' that, but it weren't no use. Joshua says, send for Heathcote. He can do such things, he says, and tells us how you'd laid a ghost out Rowsley way, an' it never came back. But t'vicar wouldn't have it. Beggin' your pardon . . .' and here the man drew back like the others, glancing up at Heathcote guiltily, '. . . he said that you were . . . he said . . .'

'I can imagine what that Godless man has said about me.'

Yes, his voice was exactly that of an actor on a stage—a somewhat unconvincing actor at that, though, to judge by their faces, the villagers had been riveted by his performance.

'My children,' he boomed again, sawing the air with his arm, like Hamlet's player king, 'I hope I have not come too late. You understand my terms?'

No one seemed to know what he meant by 'terms'. There was an embarrassed silence.

'Terms? What's he mean, "terms"?' someone near to me whispered.

'I think he means the money,' I supplied.

'We took up a collection, Mester Heathcote,' shouted another.

'It's t'full amount.'

This appeared to satisfy Heathcote, who drew himself up to his full height, and seemed to be about to launch into the main part of his performance.

'I must demand that you remain still!' he intoned. 'Quite still, and make not a sound. No one must enter the circle that I have made!'

Then he turned away from his audience and disappeared behind the broad trunk of the oak. He returned a moment later with a strange apparatus, a framework of spidery wooden paths joined to form a kind of wall-less tent, which he assembled in the centre of the circle. When it was complete it formed the shape of a sort of five-pointed star. A pentacle. He reminded me at that moment, with his purple cloth, his magic circle of candles, which no one was allowed to enter, his pentacle, of a cheap conjuror in a side show or at a children's party.

He knelt before his framework then and began a sort of prayer. His arms thrust towards to the sky, his head was thrown back. He stayed in this bizarre posture for some twenty minutes, so that I became very bored and irritated, and cold, and thought longingly of the cosy fire at the inn.

'What's happening? What's going on?' voices whispered around me. It seemed that they were more impressed by this display that I was.

'He's so *still*!'

'Not even breathing . . .'

'He *is*, there's his breath look . . .'

'Not like prayin' somehow . . .'

'I don't like it. I'm afeared.'

Then, after so much silence, a sound. A disagreeable droning chant began to emerge from Heathcote's lips. An alien language, a strange chanting.

'Berald Berald Berald
Balbin Balbin Balbin
Gab gabor agaba
Gab gabor agaba . . .'

The words were familiar to me. In my studies of the occult and its rituals I had come across them many times. They were reputed to have a peculiar power and importance. It seemed that I had underestimated Heathcote.

The villagers, however, had made no such mistake. And now

their faith was, in a sense, rewarded.

In the centre of the circle, under the shelter of the pentacle framework, a silver mist gathered. It shone very low on the grass, gradually becoming clearer, sharper, more solid.

It was a fish. About the size of a large salmon, but of a silvery brightness that has never been known in any earthly river or sea. It bore about it a shimmering halo of brightness. We gazed at it in utter disbelief.

It was only once I had grown accustomed to the creature's brightness that I observed that it appeared to be breathing, in the heavy desperate manner of any landed fish drowning in the air.

It began to move. Have you ever seen a landed fish try to get back to the water that is its natural element and home? How it twists and turns its body like a frantic snake, how it struggles and fights with the air and the earth for its life? Just so did the apparition struggle forward through the grass, twisting and writhing. Its progress was painfully slow, and soon its gasping became louder and the jack-knife movements of its silvery body more frantic still. The water it was seeking lay across the field—a spring and a brook known as Lumb Mouth.

The villagers broke their circle as the fish flapped near them. Then a horrible thing happened. In its agony, the fish opened its mouth and from between its jaws came a sound that I hope I shall one day be able to forget—the sound of the piteous crying of a five-year-old girl.

The villagers heard it too. Some broke down and wept. The woman from the inn, Betty, shouted aloud:

'It's her voice! That's Annie's voice! What have you done to her?' she screamed, turning on Heathcote. 'You devil, what have you done?'

But still no one dared to enter the circle.

Heathcote himself was still kneeling. He appeared to have completely lost his reason. He continued to gabble the words of his incantation automatically, like a clock that is winding down but cannot yet stop. His eyes stared and his jaw gaped. I have never seen a man so terrified.

'Gab gabor agaba . . . Gab gabor agaba . . .'

Several folk broke into the circle then and rushed forward to pick up the fish, to run with it across the field to the water. But before they could lay their hands on it a voice cried out from across the field:

'No, do not help her! She must make her own way! That is the only way to save her!'

A man in a cleric's surplice and gown had come into the field, bearded, impressive, glaring at his people in a mixture of anger and grief, fierce tears standing in his eyes.

'Listen to me!' he shouted at them. 'Listen to me for once! This foolish man . . . ach, what can I say . . .

'Yes, you're right Betty, it's Annie, or a part of her, and she is in hell now for your faithlessness. She is climbing, brave creature that she is, out of the very pit of hell itself. But we may not help her. She can only make this journey by herself!'

And so we stood and watched, as the fish continued its labour, its terrible suffering progress across the grass. Sometimes it hardly seemed to be moving forward at all, though it twisted and wrenched its body from side to side. It took a whole hour for the fish to reach the bank of the brook. It paused there, a smear of silver against the muddy banks, then twisted its body once more and fell into the stream. The tension snapped. Many of the women broke down and wept.

But one said that she turned and looked down towards the river, and saw a white bird fly out of the water and soar into the sky to perch at length amongst the bare branches of the Edwin tree. But no-one else can confirm her story.

James H. Schmitz

Grandpa

A green-winged downy thing as big as a hen fluttered along the hillside to a point directly above Cord's head and hovered there, twenty feet above him. Cord, a fifteen-year-old human being, leaned back against a skipboat parked on the equator of a world that had known human beings for only the past four Earth-years, and eyed the thing speculatively. The thing was, in the free and easy terminology of the Sutang Colonial Team, a swamp bug. Concealed in the downy fur behind the bug's head was a second, smaller, semi-parasitical thing, classed as a bug rider.

The bug itself looked like a new species to Cord. Its parasite might or might not turn out to be another unknown. Cord was a natural research man; his first glimpse of the odd flying team had sent endless curiosities thrilling through him. How did that particular phenomenon tick, and *why*? What fascinating things, once you'd learned about it, could you get it to *do*?

Normally, he was hampered by circumstances in carrying out any such investigation. Junior colonial students like Cord were expected to confine their curiosity to the pattern of research set up by the Station to which they were attached. Cord's inclination towards independent experiments had got him into disfavour with his immediate superiors before this.

He sent a casual glance in the direction of the Yoger Bay Colonial Station behind him. No signs of human activity about that low, fortresslike bulk in the hill. Its central lock was still closed. In fifteen minutes, it was scheduled to be opened to let out the Planetary Regent, who was inspecting the Yoger Bay Station and its principal activities today.

Fifteen minutes was time enough to find out something about the new bug, Cord decided.

But he'd have to collect it first.

He slid out one of the two handguns holstered at his side. This one was his own property: a Vanadian projectile weapon. Cord thumbed it to position for anaesthetic small-game missiles and brought the hovering swamp bug down, drilled neatly and microscopically through the head.

As the bug hit the ground, the rider left its back. A tiny scarlet demon, round and bouncy as a rubber ball, it shot towards Cord in three long hops, mouth wide to sink home inch-long, venom-dripping fangs. Rather breathlessly, Cord triggered the gun again and knocked it out in mid-leap. A new species, all right! Most bug riders were harmless plant eaters, mere suckers of vegetable juice—

'Cord!' A feminine voice.

Cord swore softly. He hadn't heard the central lock click open. She must have come around from the other side of the station.

'Hello, Grayan!' he shouted innocently without looking round. 'Come and see what I've got! New species!'

Grayan Mahoney, a slender, black-haired girl two years older than himself, came trotting down the hillside towards him. She was Sutang's star colonial student, and the station manager, Nirmond, indicated from time to time that she was a fine example for Cord to pattern his own behaviour on. In spite of that, she and Cord were good friends.

'Cord, you idiot,' she scowled as she came up. 'Stop playing the collector! If the Regent came out now, you'd be sunk. Nirmond's been telling her about you!'

'Telling her what?' Cord asked, startled.

'For one thing,' Grayan reported, 'that you don't keep up on your assigned work.'

'Golly!' gulped Cord, dismayed.

'Golly, is right! I keep warning you!'

'What'll I do?'

'Start acting as if you had good sense mainly.' Grayan grinned suddenly. 'But if you mess up our tour of the Bay Farms today, you'll be off the Team for good!'

She turned to go. 'You might as well put the skipboat back; we're not using it. Nirmond's driving us down to the edge of the bay in a treadcar, and we'll take a raft from there.'

Leaving his newly bagged specimens to revive by themselves and flutter off again, Cord hurriedly flew the skipboat around the station and rolled it back into its stall.

Three rafts lay moored just offshore in the marshy cove at the edge of which Nirmond had stopped the treadcar. They looked somewhat like exceptionally broad-brimmed, well-worn sugarloaf hats floating out there, green and leathery. Or like lily pads twenty-five feet across, with the upper section of a big, grey-green pineapple growing from the centre of each. Plant animals of some sort. Sutang was too new to have had its phyla sorted out into anything remotely like an orderly classification. The rafts were a local oddity which had been investigated and could be regarded as harmless and moderately useful. Their usefulness lay in the fact that they were employed as a rather slow means of transportation about the shallow, swampy waters of the Yoger Bay. That was as far as the Team's interest in them went at present.

The Regent stood up from the back seat of the car, where she was sitting next to Cord. There were only four in the party; Grayan was up front with Nirmond.

'Are those our vehicles?' The Regent sounded amused.

Nirmond grinned. 'Don't underestimate them, Dane! They could become an important economic factor in this region in time. But, as a matter of fact, these three are smaller than I like to use.' He was peering about the reedy edges of the cove. 'There's a regular monster parked here usually—'

Grayan turned to Cord. 'Maybe Cord knows where Grandpa is hiding.'

It was well-meant, but Cord had been hoping nobody would ask him about Grandpa. Now they all looked at him.

'Oh, you want Grandpa?' he said, somewhat flustered. 'Well, I left him . . . I mean I saw him a couple of weeks ago about a mile south from here—'

Nirmond grunted and told the Regent, 'The rafts tend to stay wherever they're left, providing it's shallow and muddy. They use a hair-root system to draw chemicals and microscopic nourishment directly from the bottom of the bay. Well—Grayan, would you like to drive us there?'

Cord settled back unhappily as the treadcar lurched into motion. Nirmond suspected he'd used Grandpa for one of his unauthorized tours of the area, and Nirmond was quite right.

'I understand you're an expert with these rafts, Cord,' Dane said from beside him. 'Grayan told me we couldn't find a better steersman, or pilot, or whatever you call it, for our trip today.'

'I can handle them,' Cord said, perspiring. 'They don't give you any trouble!' He didn't feel he'd made a good impression on the Regent so far. Dane was a young, handsome-looking woman with an easy way of talking and laughing, but she wasn't the head of the Sutang Colonial Team for nothing.

'There's one big advantage our beasties have over a skip-boat, too,' Nirmond remarked from the front seat. 'You don't have to worry about a snapper trying to climb on board with you!' He went on to describe the stinging ribbon-tentacles the rafts spread around them under the water to discourage creatures that might make a meal off their tender underparts. The snappers and two or three other active and aggressive species of the bay hadn't yet learned it was foolish to attack armed human beings in a boat, but they would skitter hurriedly out of the path of a leisurely perambulating raft.

Cord was happy to be ignored for the moment. The Regent, Nirmond, and Grayan were all Earth people, which was true of most of the members of the Team; and Earth people made him uncomfortable, particularly in groups. Vanadia, his own home world, had barely graduated from the status of Earth colony itself, which might explain the difference.

The treadcar swung around and stopped, and Grayan stood up in the front seat, pointing. 'That's Grandpa, over there!'

Dane also stood up and whistled softly, apparently impressed by Grandpa's fifty-foot spread. Cord looked around in surprise. He was pretty sure this was several hundred yards from the spot where he'd left the big raft two weeks ago; and, as Nirmond said, they didn't usually move about by themselves.

Puzzled, he followed the others down a narrow path to the water, hemmed in by tree-sized reeds. Now and then he got a glimpse of Grandpa's swimming platform, the rim of which just touched the shore. Then the path opened out, and he saw the whole raft lying in sunlit, shallow water; and he stopped short, startled.

Nirmond was about to step up on the platform, ahead of Dane.

'Wait!' Cord shouted. His voice sounded squeaky with alarm. 'Stop!'

He came running forward.

'What's the matter, Cord?' Nirmond's voice was quiet and urgent.

'Don't get on that raft—it's changed!' Cord's voice sounded wobbly, even to himself. 'Maybe it's not even Grandpa—'

He saw he was wrong on the last point before he'd finished the sentence. Scattered along the rim of the raft were discoloured spots left by a variety of heat-guns, one of which had been his own. It was the way you goaded the sluggish and mindless things into motion. Cord pointed at the cone-shaped central projection. 'There—his head! He's sprouting!'

Grandpa's head, as befitted his girth, was almost twelve feet high and equally wide. It was armour-plated like the back of a saurian to keep off plant suckers, but two weeks ago it had been an otherwise featureless knob, like those on all other rafts. Now scores of long, kinky, leafless vines had grown out from all surfaces of the cone, like green wires. Some were drawn up like tightly coiled springs, others trailed limply to the platform and over it. The top of the cone was dotted with angry red buds, rather like pimples, which hadn't been there before either. Grandpa looked unhealthy.

'Well,' Nirmond said, 'so it is. Sprouting!' Grayan made a choked sound. Nirmond glanced at Cord as if puzzled. 'Is that all that was bothering you, Cord?'

'Well, sure!' Cord began excitedly. He had caught the significance of the word 'all'; his hackles were still up, and he was shaking. 'None of them ever—'

Then he stopped. He could tell by their faces, that they hadn't got it. Or rather, that they'd got it all right but simply weren't going to let it change their plans. The rafts were classified as harmless, according to the Regulations. Until proved otherwise, they would continue to be regarded as harmless. You didn't waste time quibbling with the Regulations—even if you were the Planetary Regent. You didn't feel you had the time to waste.

He tried again. 'Look—' he began. What he wanted to tell them was that Grandpa with one unknown factor added wasn't Grandpa any more. He was an unpredictable, oversized life form, to be investigated with cautious thoroughness till you knew what the unknown factor meant. He stared at them helplessly.

Dane turned to Nirmond. 'Perhaps you'd better check,' she said. She didn't add, '—to reassure the boy!' but that was what she meant.

Cord felt himself flushing. But there was nothing he could say or do now except watch Nirmond walk steadily across the platform. Grandpa shivered slightly a few times, but the rafts always did that when someone first stepped on them. The station manager stopped before one of the kinky sprouts, touched it, and then gave it a tug. He reached up and poked at the lowest of the budlike growths. 'Odd-looking things!' he called back. He gave Cord another glance. 'Well, everything seems harmless enough, Cord. Coming aboard, everyone?'

It was like dreaming a dream in which you yelled and yelled at people and couldn't make them hear you! Cord stepped up stiff-

legged on the platform behind Dane and Grayan. He knew exactly what would have happened if he'd hesitated even a moment.
One of them would have said in a friendly voice, careful not to let
it sound contemptuous: 'You don't have to come along if you
don't want to, Cord!'

Grayan had unholstered her heat-gun and was ready to start
Grandpa moving out into the channels of the Yoger Bay.

Cord hauled out his own heat-gun and said roughly, 'I was to
do that!'

'All right, Cord.' She gave him a brief, impersonal smile and
stood aside.

They were so infuriatingly polite!

For a while, Cord almost hoped that something awesome and
catastrophic would happen promptly to teach the Team people
a lesson. But nothing did. As always, Grandpa shook himself
vaguely and experimentally when he felt the heat on one edge of
the platform and then decided to withdraw from it, all of which
was standard procedure. Under the water, out of sight, were the
raft's working sections: short, thick leaf-structures shaped like
paddles and designed to work as such, along with the slimy
nettle-streamers which kept the vegetarians of the Yoger Bay
away, and a jungle of hair roots through which Grandpa sucked
nourishment from the mud and the sluggish waters of the bay and
with which he also anchored himself.

The paddles started churning, the platform quivered, the hair
roots were hauled out of the mud; and Grandpa was on his
ponderous way.

Cord switched off the heat, reholstered his gun, and stood up.
Once in motion, the rafts tended to keep travelling unhurriedly
for quite a while. To stop them, you gave them a touch of heat
along their leading edge; and they could be turned in any direction
by using the gun lightly on the opposite side of the platform. It was
simple enough.

Cord didn't look at the others. He was still burning inside.
He watched the reed beds move past and open out, giving him
glimpses of the misty, yellow and green and blue expanses of the
brackish bay ahead. Behind the mist, to the west, were the Yoger
Straits, tricky and ugly water when the tides were running; and
beyond the Straits lay the open sea, the great Zlanti Deep, which
was another world entirely and one of which he hadn't seen much
as yet.

Grayan called from beside Dane, 'What's the best route from

here into the farms, Cord?'

'The big channel to the right,' he answered. He added somewhat sullenly, 'We're headed for it!'

Grayan came over to him. 'The Regent doesn't want to see all of it,' she said, lowering her voice. 'The algae and plankton beds first. Then as much of the mutated grains as we can show her in about three hours. Steer for the ones that have been doing best, and you'll keep Nirmond happy!'

She gave him a conspiratorial wink. Cord looked after her uncertainly. You couldn't tell from her behaviour that anything was wrong. Maybe—

He had a flare of hope. It was hard not to like the Team people, even when they were being rock-headed about their Regulations. Anyway, the day wasn't over yet. He might still redeem himself in the Regent's opinion.

Cord had a sudden cheerful, if improbable vision of some bay monster plunging up on the raft with snapping jaws; and of himself alertly blowing out what passed for the monster's brains before anyone else—Nirmond in particular—was even aware of the threat. The bay monsters shunned Grandpa, of course, but there might be ways of tempting one of them.

So far, Cord realized, he'd been letting his feelings control him. It was time to start thinking!

Grandpa first. So he'd sprouted—green vines and red buds, purpose unknown, but with no change observable in his behaviour-patterns otherwise. He was the biggest raft in this end of the bay, though all of them had been growing steadily in the two years since Cord had first seen one. Sutang's seasons changed slowly; its year was somewhat more than five Earth-years long. The first Team members to land here hadn't seen a full year pass.

Grandpa then was showing a seasonal change. The other rafts, not quite so far developed, would be reacting similarly a little later. Plant animals—they might be blossoming, preparing to propagate.

'Grayan,' he called, 'how do the rafts get started? When they're small, I mean.'

'Nobody knows yet,' she said. 'We were just talking about it. About half of the coastal marsh-fauna of the continent seems to go through a preliminary larval stage in the sea.' She nodded at the red buds on the raft's cone. 'It *looks* as if Grandpa is going to produce flowers and let the wind or tide take the seeds out through the Straits.'

It made sense. It also knocked out Cord's still half-held hope that the change in Grandpa might turn out to be drastic enough, in some way, to justify his reluctance to get on board. Cord studied Grandpa's armoured head carefully once more—unwilling to give up that hope entirely. There were a series of vertical gummy black slits between the armour plates, which hadn't been in evidence two weeks ago either. It looked as if Grandpa was beginning to come apart at the seams. Which might indicate that the rafts, big as they grew to be, didn't outlive a full seasonal cycle, but came to flower at about this time of Sutang's year, and died. However, it was a safe bet that Grandpa wasn't going to collapse into senile decay before they completed their trip today.

Cord gave up on Grandpa. The other notion returned to him— Perhaps he *could* coax an obliging bay monster into action that would show the Regent he was no sissy!

Because the monsters were there all right.

Kneeling at the edge of the platform and peering down into the wine-coloured, clear water of the deep channel they were moving through, Cord could see a fair selection of them at almost any moment.

Some five or six snappers, for one thing. Like big, flattened cray-fish, chocolate-brown mostly, with green and red spots on their carapaced backs. In some areas they were so thick you'd wonder what they found to live on, except that they ate almost anything, down to chewing up the mud in which they squatted. However, they preferred their food in large chunks and alive, which was one reason you didn't go swimming in the bay. They would attack a boat on occasion; but the excited manner in which the ones he saw were scuttling off towards the edges of the channel showed they wanted nothing to do with a big moving raft.

Dotted across the bottom were two-foot round holes which looked vacant at the moment. Normally, Cord knew, there would be a head filling each of those holes. The heads consisted mainly of triple sets of jaws, held open patiently like so many traps to grab at anything that came within range of the long wormlike bodies behind the heads. But Grandpa's passage, waving his stingers like transparent pennants through the water, had scared the worms out of sight, too.

Otherwise, mostly schools of small stuff—and then a flash of wicked scarlet, off to the left behind the raft, darting out from the reeds, turning its needle-nose into their wake.

Cord watched it without moving. He knew that creature, though it was rare in the bay and hadn't been classified. Swift, vicious—alert enough to snap swamp bugs out of the air as they fluttered across the surface. And he'd tantalized one with fishing tackle once into leaping up on a moored raft, where it had flung itself about furiously until he was able to shoot it.

'What fantastic creatures!' Dane's voice just behind him.

'Yellowheads,' said Nirmond. 'They've got a high utility rating. Keep down the bugs.'

Cord stood up casually. It was no time for tricks! The reed bed to their right was thick with Yellowheads, a colony of them. Vaguely froggy things, man sized and better. Of all the creatures he'd discovered in the bay, Cord liked them least. The flabby, sack-like bodies clung with four thin limbs to the upper section of the twenty-foot reeds that lined the channel. They hardly ever moved, but their huge bulging eyes seemed to take in everything that went on about them. Every so often, a downy swamp bug came close enough; and a Yellowhead would open its vertical, enormous, tooth-lined slash of a mouth, extend the whole front of its face like a bellows in a flashing strike; and the bug would be gone. They might be useful, but Cord hated them.

'Ten years from now we should know what the cycle of coastal life is like,' Nirmond said. 'When we set up the Yoger Bay Station there were no Yellowheads here. They came the following year. Still with traces of the oceanic larval form; but the metamorphosis was almost complete. About twelve inches long—'

Dane remarked that the same pattern was duplicated endlessly elsewhere. The Regent was inspecting the Yellowhead colony with field glasses; she put them down now, looked at Cord, and smiled, 'How far to the farms?'

'About twenty minutes.'

'The key,' Nirmond said, 'seems to be the Zlanti Basin. It must be almost a soup of life in spring.'

'It is,' nodded Dane, who had been here in Sutang's spring, four Earth-years ago. 'It's beginning to look as if the Basin alone might justify colonization. The question is still'—she gestured towards the Yellowheads—'how do creatures like that get here?'

They walked off towards the other side of the raft, arguing about ocean currents. Cord might have followed. But something splashed back of them, off to the left and not too far back. He stayed, watching.

After a moment, he saw the big Yellowhead. It had slipped down from its reedy perch, which was what had caused the splash. Almost submerged at the water line, it stared after the raft with huge, pale-green eyes. To Cord, it seemed to look directly at him. In that moment, he knew for the first time why he didn't like Yellowheads. There was something very like intelligence in that look, an alien calculation. In creatures like that, intelligence seemed out of place. What use could they have for it?

A little shiver went over him when it sank completely under the water and he realized it intended to swim after the raft. But it was mostly excitement. He had never seen a Yellowhead come down out of the reeds before. The obliging monster he'd been looking for might be presenting itself in an unexpected way.

Half a minute later, he watched it again, swimming awkwardly far down. It had no immediate intention of boarding, at any rate. Cord saw it come into the area of the raft's trailing stingers. It manoeuvred its way between them, with curiously human swimming motions, and went out of sight under the platform.

He stood up, wondering what it meant. The Yellowhead had appeared to know about the stingers; there had been an air of purpose in every move of its approach. He was tempted to tell the others about it, but there was the moment of triumph he could have if it suddenly came slobbering up over the edge of the platform and he nailed it before their eyes.

It was almost time anyway to turn the raft in towards the farms. If nothing happened before then—

He watched. Almost five minutes, but no sign of the Yellowhead. Still wondering, a little uneasy, he gave Grandpa a calculated needling of heat.

After a moment, he repeated it. Then he drew a deep breath and forgot all about the Yellowhead.

'Nirmond!' he called sharply.

The three of them were standing near the centre of the platform, next to the big armoured cone, looking ahead at the farms. They glanced around.

'What's the matter now, Cord?'

Cord couldn't say it for a moment. He was suddenly, terribly scared again. Something *had* gone wrong!

'The raft won't turn!' he told them.

'Give it a real burn this time!' Nirmond said.

Cord glanced up at him. Nirmond, standing a few steps in front of Dane and Grayan as if he wanted to protect them, had begun to look a little strained, and no wonder. Cord already had pressed the gun to three different points on the platform; but Grandpa appeared to have developed a sudden anaesthesia for heat. They kept moving steadily towards the centre of the bay.

Now Cord held his breath, switched the heat on full, and let Grandpa have it. A six-inch patch on the platform blistered up instantly, turned brown, then black—

Grandpa stopped dead. Just like that.

'That's right! Keep burn—' Nirmond didn't finish his order.

A giant shudder. Cord staggered back towards the water. Then the whole edge of the raft came curling up behind him and went down again smacking the bay with a sound like a cannon shot. He flew forward off his feet, hit the platform face down, and flattened himself against it. It swelled up beneath him. Two more enormous slaps and joltings. Then quiet. He looked round for the others.

He lay within twelve feet of the central cone. Some twenty or thirty of the mysterious new vines the cone had sprouted were stretched stiffly towards him now, like so many thin green fingers. They couldn't quite reach him. The nearest tip was still ten inches from his shoes.

But Grandpa had caught the others, all three of them. They were tumbled together at the foot of the cone, wrapped in a stiff network of green vegetable ropes, and they didn't move.

Cord drew his feet up cautiously, prepared for another earthquake reaction. But nothing happened. Then he discovered that Grandpa was back in motion on his previous course. The heat-gun had vanished. Gently, he took out the Vanadian gun.

A voice, thin and pain-filled, spoke to him from one of the three huddled bodies.

'Cord? It didn't get you?' It was the Regent.

'No,' he said, keeping his voice low. He realized suddenly he'd simply assumed they were all dead. Now he felt sick and shaky.

'What are you doing?'

Cord looked at Grandpa's big, armour-plated head with a certain hunger. The cones were hollowed out inside, the station's lab had decided their chief function was to keep enough air trapped under the rafts to float them. But in that central section was also the organ that controlled Grandpa's overall reactions.

He said softly, 'I have a gun and twelve heavy-duty explosive bullets. Two of them will blow that cone apart.'

'No good, Cord!' the pain-racked voice told him: 'If the thing sinks, we'll die anyway. You have anaesthetic charges for that gun of yours?'

He stared at her back. 'Yes.'

'Give Nirmond and the girl a shot each, before you do anything else. Directly into the spine, if you can. But don't come any closer—'

Somehow, Cord couldn't argue with that voice. He stood up carefully. The gun made two soft spitting sounds.

'All right,' he said hoarsely. 'What do I do now?'

Dane was silent a moment. 'I'm sorry, Cord, I can't tell you that. I'll tell you what I can—'

She paused for some seconds again.

'This thing didn't try to kill us, Cord. It could have easily. It's incredibly strong. I saw it break Nirmond's legs. But as soon as we stopped moving, it just held us. They were both unconscious then—'

'You've got that to go on. It was trying to pitch you within reach of its vines or tendrils, or whatever they are, too, wasn't it?'

'I think so,' Cord said shakily. That was what had happened, of course; and at any moment Grandpa might try again.

'Now it's feeding us some sort of anaesthetic of its own through those vines. Tiny thorns. A sort of numbness—' Dane's voice trailed off a moment. Then she said clearly, 'Look, Cord—it seems we're food it's storing up! You get that?'

'Yes,' he said.

'Seeding time for the rafts. There are analogues. Live food for its seed probably; not for the raft. One couldn't have counted on that. Cord?'

'Yes, I'm here.'

'I want,' said Dane, 'to stay awake as long as I can. But there's really just one other thing—this raft's going somewhere, to some particularly favourable location. And that might be very near shore. You might make it in then; otherwise it's up to you. But keep your head and wait for a chance. No heroics, understand?'

'Sure, I understand,' Cord told her. He realized then that he was talking reassuringly, as if it wasn't the Planetary Regent but someone like Grayan.

'Nirmond's the worst,' Dane said. 'The girl was knocked unconscious at once. If it weren't for my arm—but, if we can get help in five hours or so, everything should be all right. Let me know if anything happens, Cord.'

'I will,' Cord said gently again. Then he sighted his gun carefully at a point between Dane's shoulder-blades, and the anaesthetic chamber made its soft, spitting sound once more. Dane's taut body relaxed slowly, and that was all.

There was no point Cord could see in letting her stay awake; because they weren't going anywhere near shore. The reed beds and the channels were already behind them, and Grandpa hadn't changed direction by the fraction of a degree. He was moving out into the open bay—and he was picking up company!

So far, Cord could count seven big rafts within two miles of them; and on the three that were closest he could make out a sprouting of new green vines. All of them were travelling in a straight direction; and the common point they were all headed for appeared to be the roaring centre of the Yoger Straits, now some three miles away!

Behind the Straits, the cold Zlanti Deep—the rolling fogs, and the open sea! It might be seeding time for the rafts, but it looked as if they weren't going to distribute their seeds in the bay . . .

Cord was a fine swimmer. He had a gun and he had a knife; in spite of what Dane had said, he might have stood a chance among the killers of the bay. But it would be a very small chance, at best. And it wasn't, he thought, as if there weren't still other possibilities. He was going to keep his head.

Except by accident, of course, nobody was going to come looking for them in time to do any good. If anyone did look, it would be around the Bay Farms. There were a number of rafts moored there; and it would be assumed they'd used one of them. Now and then something unexpected happened and somebody simply vanished; by the time it was figured out just what had happened on this occasion, it would be much too late.

Neither was anybody likely to notice within the next few hours that the rafts had started migrating out of the swamps through the Yoger Straits. There was a small weather station a little inland, on the north side of the Straits, which used a helicopter occasionally. It was about as improbable, Cord decided dismally, that they'd use it in the right spot just now as it would be for a jet transport to happen to come in low enough to spot them.

The fact that it was up to him, as the Regent had said, sank in a little more after that!

Simply because he was going to try it sooner or later, he carried out an experiment next that he knew couldn't work. He opened the gun's anaesthetic chamber and counted out fifty pellets—rather hurriedly because he didn't particularly want to think of what he might be using them for eventually. There were around three hundred charges left in the chamber then; and in the next few minutes Cord carefully planted a third of them in Grandpa's head.

He stopped after that. A whale might have showed signs of somnolence under a lesser load. Grandpa paddled on undisturbed. Perhaps he had become a little numb in spots, but his cells weren't equipped to distribute the soporific effect of that type of drug.

There wasn't anything else Cord could think of doing before they reached the Straits. At the rate they were moving, he calculated that would happen in something less than an hour; and if they did pass through the Straits, he was going to risk a swim. He didn't think Dane would have disapproved, under the circumstances. If the raft simply carried them all out into the foggy vastness of the Zlanti Deep, there would be no practical chance of survival left at all.

Meanwhile, Grandpa was definitely picking up speed. And there were other changes going on—minor ones, but still a little awe-inspiring to Cord. The pimply-looking red buds that dotted the upper part of the cone were opening out gradually. From the centre of most of them protruded something like a thin, wet, scarlet worm: a worm that twisted weakly, extended itself by an inch or so, rested, and twisted again, and stretched up a little farther, groping into the air. The vertical black slits between the armour plates looked deeper and wider than they had been even some minutes ago; a dark, thick liquid dripped slowly from several of them.

In other circumstances Cord knew he would have been fascinated by these developments in Grandpa. As it was, they drew his suspicious attention only because he didn't know what they meant.

Then something quite horrible happened suddenly. Grayan started moaning loudly and terribly and twisted almost completely around. Afterwards, Cord knew it hadn't been a second before he stopped her struggles and the sounds together with another anaesthetic pellet; but the vines had tightened their grip on her first, not flexibly but like the digging, bony, green talons of some monstrous bird of prey.

White and sweating, Cord put his gun down slowly while the vines relaxed again. Grayan didn't seem to have suffered any additional harm; and she would certainly have been the first to point out that his murderous rage might have been as intelligently directed against a machine. But for some moments Cord continued to luxuriate furiously in the thought that, at any instant he chose, he could still turn the raft very quickly into a ripped and exploded mess of sinking vegetation.

Instead, and more sensibly, he gave both Dane and Nirmond another shot, to prevent a similar occurrence with them. The contents of two such pellets, he knew, would keep any human being torpid for at least four hours.

Cord withdrew his mind hastily from the direction it was turning into; but it wouldn't stay withdrawn. The thought kept coming up again, until at last he had to recognize it.

Five shots would leave the three of them completely unconscious whatever else might happen to them, until they either died from other causes or were given a counteracting agent.

Shocked, he told himself he couldn't do it. It was exactly like killing them.

But then, quite steadily, he found himself raising the gun once more, to bring the total charge for each of the three Team people up to five.

Barely thirty minutes later, he watched a raft as big as the one he rode go sliding into the foaming white waters of the Straits a few hundred yards ahead, and dart off abruptly at an angle, caught by one of the swirling currents. It pitched and spun, made some headway, and was swept aside again. And then it righted itself once more. Not like some blindly animated vegetable, Cord thought, but like a creature that struggled with intelligent purpose to maintain its chosen direction.

At least, they seemed practically unsinkable . . .

Knife in hand, he flattened himself against the platform as the Straits roared just ahead. When the platform jolted and tilted up beneath him, he rammed the knife all the way into it and hung on. Cold water rushed suddenly over him, and Grandpa shuddered like a labouring engine. In the middle of it all, Cord had the horrified notion that the raft might release its unconscious human prisoners in its struggle with the Straits. But he underestimated Grandpa in that. Grandpa also hung on.

Abruptly, it was over. They were riding a long swell, and there were three other rafts not far away. The Straits had swept them together, but they seemed to have no interest in one another's company. As Cord stood up shakily and began to strip off his clothes, they were visibly drawing apart again. The platform of one of them was half-submerged; it must have lost too much of the air that held it afloat and, like a small ship, it was foundering.

From this point, it was only a two-mile swim to the shore north of the Straits, and another mile inland from there to the Straits Head Station. He didn't know about the current; but the distance didn't seem too much, and he couldn't bring himself to leave knife and gun behind. The bay creatures loved warmth and mud, they didn't venture beyond the Straits. But Zlanti Deep bred its own killers, though they weren't often observed so close to shore.

Things were beginning to look rather hopeful.

Thin, crying voices drifted overhead, like the voices of curious cats, as Cord knotted his clothes into a tight bundle, shoes inside. He looked up. There were four of them circling there; magnified sea-going swamp bugs, each carrying an unseen rider. Probably harmless scavengers—but the ten-foot wingspread was impressive. Uneasily, Cord remembered the venomously carnivorous rider he'd left lying beside the station.

One of them dipped lazily and came sliding down towards him. It soared overhead and came back, to hover about the raft's cone.

The bug rider that directed the mindless flier hadn't been interested in him at all! Grandpa was baiting it!

Cord stared in fascination. The top of the cone was alive now with a softly wriggling mass of the scarlet, wormlike extrusions that had started sprouting before the raft left the bay. Presumably, they looked enticingly edible to the bug rider.

The flier settled with an airy fluttering and touched the cone. Like a trap springing shut, the green vines flashed up and around it, crumpling the brittle wings, almost vanishing into the long, soft body!

Barely a second later, Grandpa made another catch, this one from the sea itself. Cord had a fleeting glimpse of something like a small, rubbery seal that flung itself out of the water upon the edge of the raft, with a suggestion of desperate haste—and was flipped on instantly against the cone where the vines clamped it down beside the flier's body.

It wasn't the enormous ease with which the unexpected kill was accomplished that left Cord standing there, completely shocked. It was the shattering of his hopes to swim ashore from here. Fifty yards away, the creature from which the rubbery thing had been fleeing showed briefly on the surface, as it turned away from the raft; and that glance was all he needed. The ivory-white body and gaping jaws were similar enough to those of the sharks of Earth to indicate the pursuer's nature. The important difference was that wherever the White Hunters of the Zlanti Deep went, they went by the thousands.

Stunned by that incredible piece of bad luck, still clutching his bundled clothes, Cord stared towards shore. Knowing what to look for, he could spot the tell-tale rollings of the surface now—the long, ivory gleams that flashed through the swells and vanished again. Shoals of smaller things burst into the air in sprays of glittering desperation, and fell back.

He would have been snapped up like a drowning fly before he'd covered a twentieth of that distance!

Grandpa was beginning to eat.

Each of the dark slits down the sides of the cone was a mouth. So far only one of them was in operating condition, and the raft wasn't able to open that one very wide as yet. The first morsel had been fed into it, however: the bug rider the vines had plucked out of the flier's downy neck fur. It took Grandpa several minutes to work it out of sight, small as it was. But it was a start.

Cord didn't feel quite sane any more. He sat there, clutching his bundle of clothes and only vaguely aware of the fact that he was shivering steadily under the cold spray that touched him now and then, while he followed Grandpa's activities attentively. He decided it would be at least some hours before one of that black set of mouths grew flexible and vigorous enough to dispose of a human being. Under the circumstances, it couldn't make much difference to the other human beings here; but the moment Grandpa reached for the first of them would also be the moment he finally blew the raft to pieces. The White Hunters were cleaner eaters, at any rate; and that was about the extent to which he could still control what was going to happen.

Meanwhile, there was the very faint chance that the weather station's helicopter might spot them.

Meanwhile also, in a weary and horrified fascination, he kept debating the mystery of what could have produced such a nightmarish change in the rafts. He could guess where they were going by now; there were scattered strings of them stretching back to the Straits or roughly parallel to their own course, and the direction was that of the plankton-swarming pool of the Zlanti Basin, a thousand miles to the north. Given time, even mobile lily pads like the rafts had been could make that trip for the benefit of their seedlings. But nothing in their structure explained the sudden change into alert and capable carnivores.

He watched the rubbery little seal-thing being hauled up to a mouth. The vines broke its neck; and the mouth took it in up to the shoulders and then went on working patiently at what was still a trifle too large a bite. Meanwhile, there were more thin cat-cries overhead; and a few minutes later, two more sea-bugs were trapped almost simultaneously and added to the larder. Grandpa dropped the dead sea-thing and fed himself another bug rider. The second rider left its mount with a sudden hop, sank its teeth viciously into one of the vines that caught it again, and was promptly battered to death against the platform.

Cord felt a resurge of unreasoning hatred against Grandpa. Killing a bug was about equal to cutting a branch from a tree; they had almost no life-awareness. But the rider had aroused his partisanship because of its appearance of intelligent action—and it was in fact closer to the human scale in that feature than to the monstrous life form that had, mechanically, but quite successfully, trapped both it and the human beings. Then his thoughts drifted again; and he found himself speculating vaguely on the curious symbiosis in which the nerve systems of two creatures as dissimilar as the bugs and their riders could be linked so closely that they functioned as one organism.

Suddenly an expression of vast and stunned surprise appeared on his face.

Why—now he *knew*!

Cord stood up hurriedly, shaking with excitement, the whole plan complete in his mind. And a dozen long vines snaked instantly in the direction of his sudden motion and groped for him, taut and stretching. They couldn't reach him, but their savagely alert reaction froze Cord briefly where he was. The platform was shuddering under his feet, as if in irritation at his inaccessibility; but it couldn't be tilted up suddenly here to throw him within the grasp of the vines, as it could around the edges.

Still, it was a warning! Cord sidled gingerly around the cone till he had gained the position he wanted, which was on the forward half of the raft. And then he waited. Waited long minutes, quite motionless, until his heart stopped pounding and the irregular angry shivering of the surface of the raft-thing died away, and the last vine tendril had stopped its blind groping. It might help a lot if, for a second or two after he next started moving, Grandpa wasn't too aware of his exact whereabouts!

He looked back once to check how far they had gone by now

beyond the Straits Head Station. It couldn't, he decided, be even an hour behind them. Which was close enough, by the most pessimistic count—if everything else worked out all right! He didn't try to think out in detail what that 'everything else' could include, because there were factors that simply couldn't be calculated in advance. And he had an uneasy feeling that speculating too vividly about them might make him almost incapable of carrying out his plan.

At last, moving carefully, Cord took the knife in his left hand but left the gun holstered. He raised the tightly knotted bundle of clothes slowly over his head, balanced in his right hand. With a long, smooth motion he tossed the bundle back across the cone, almost to the opposite edge of the platform.

It hit with a soggy thump. Almost immediately, the whole far edge of the raft buckled and flapped up to toss the strange object to the reaching vines.

Simultaneously, Cord was racing forward. For a moment, his attempt to divert Grandpa's attention seemed completely successful—then he was pitched to his knees as the platform came up.

He was within eight feet of the edge. As it slapped down again, he drew himself desperately forward.

An instant later, he was knifing down through cold, clear water, just ahead of the raft, then twisting and coming up again.

The raft was passing over him. Clouds of tiny sea creatures scattered through its dark jungle of feeding roots. Cord jerked back from a broad, wavering streak of glassy greenness, which was a stinger, and felt a burning jolt on his side, which meant he'd been touched lightly by another. He bumped on blindly through the slimy black tangles of hair roots that covered the bottom of the raft; then green half-light passed over him, and he burst up into the central bubble under the cone.

Half-light and foul, hot air. Water slapped around him, dragging him away again—nothing to hang on to here! Then above him, to his right, moulded against the interior curve of the cone as if it had grown there from the start, the froglike, man-sized shape of the Yellowhead.

The raft rider!

Cord reached up, caught Grandpa's symbiotic partner and guide by a flabby hind-leg, pulled himself half out of the water and struck twice with the knife, fast, while the pale-green eyes were still opening.

He'd thought the Yellowhead might need a second or so to

detach itself from its host, as the bug riders usually did, before it tried to defend itself. This one merely turned its head; the mouth slashed down and clamped on Cord's left arm above the elbow. His right hand sank the knife through one staring eye, and the Yellowhead jerked away, pulling the knife from his grasp.

Sliding down, he wrapped both hands around the slimy leg and hauled with all his weight. For a moment more, the Yellowhead hung on. Then the countless neural extensions that connected it now with the raft came free in a succession of sucking, tearing sounds; and Cord and the Yellowhead splashed into the water together.

Black tangle of roots again—and two more electric burns suddenly across his back and legs! Strangling, Cord let go. Below him, for a moment, a body was turning over and over with oddly human motions; then a solid wall of water thrust him up and aside, as something big and white struck the turning body and went on.

Cord broke the surface twelve feet behind the raft. And that would have been that, if Grandpa hadn't already been slowing down.

After two tries, he floundered back up on the platform and lay there gasping and coughing awhile. There were no indications that his presence was resented now. A few lax vine-tips twitched uneasily, as if trying to remember previous functions, when he came limping up presently to make sure his three companions were still breathing; but Cord never noticed that.

They were still breathing; and he knew better than to waste time trying to help them himself. He took Grayan's heat-gun from its holster. Grandpa had come to a full stop.

Cord hadn't had time to become completely sane again, or he might have worried now whether Grandpa, violently sundered from his controlling partner, was still capable of motion on his own. Instead, he determined the approximate direction of the Straits Head Station, selected a corresponding spot on the platform and gave Grandpa a light tap of heat.

Nothing happened immediately. Cord sighed patiently and stepped up the heat a little.

Grandpa shuddered gently. Cord stood up. •

Slowly and hesitatingly at first, then with steadfast—though now again brainless—purpose, Grandpa began paddling back towards the Straits Head Station.

The Cold Flame

I was asleep when Patrick rang up. The bell sliced through a dream about this extraordinary jampot factory, a kind of rose-red brick catacomb, much older than time, sunk deep on top of the Downs, and I was not pleased to be woken. I groped with a blind arm and worked the receiver in between my ear and the pillow.

'Ellis? Is that you?'

'Of course it is,' I snarled. 'Who else do you expect in my bed at three a.m.? Why in heaven's name ring up at this time?'

'I'm sorry,' he said, sounding muffled and distant and apologetic. 'Where I am it's only half past something.' A sort of oceanic roar separated us for a moment, then I heard him say, '. . . rang you as soon as I could.'

'Well, where are you?'

Then I woke up a bit more and interrupted as he began speaking again. 'Hey, I thought you were supposed to be dead! There were headlines in the evening papers—a climbing accident. Was it a mistake then?'

'No, I'm dead right enough. I fell into the crater of a volcano.'

'What were you doing on a *volcano*, for goodness' sake?'

'Lying on the lip writing a poem about what it looked like inside. The bit I was lying on broke off.' Patrick sounded regretful. 'It would have been a good poem, too.'

Patrick was a poet, perhaps I should explain. Had been a poet. Or said he was. No one had ever seen his poetry because he steadfastly refused to let anybody read his work, though he insisted, with a quiet self-confidence not otherwise habitual to him, that the poems were very good indeed. In no other respect was he remarkable, but most people quite liked Patrick; he was a lanky amusing creature with guileless blue eyes and a passion for singing sad, randy songs when he had had a drink or two. For some time I had been a little in love with Patrick. I was sorry to hear he was dead.

'Look, Patrick,' I began again. 'Are you sure you're dead?'

'Of course I'm sure.'

'Where are you, then?'

'Lord knows. I've hardly had time to look round yet. There's something on my mind; that's why I contacted you.'

The word contacted seemed inappropriate. I said, 'Why ring up?'

'I could appear if you'd prefer it.'

Remembering the cause of his death I said hastily, 'No, no, let's go on as we are. What's on your mind?'

'It's my poems, Ellis. Could you get them published, do you think?'

My heart sank a bit, as anybody's does at this sort of request from a friend, but I said, 'Where are they?'

'At my flat. A big thick stack of quarto paper, all handwritten. In my desk.'

'Okay. I'll see what I can do. But listen, love—I don't want to sound a gloomy note, but suppose no publisher will touch them—what then? Promise you won't hold me responsible? Keep hanging around, you know, haunting, that kind of thing?'

'No, of course not,' he said quickly. 'But you needn't worry. Those poems are good. There's a picture at the flat as well, though, behind the wardrobe, with its face to the wall. As a matter of fact it's a portrait of my mother. It's by Chapdelaine—done before he made his name. About seven years ago I got him to paint her for her birthday present (this was before I quarrelled with Mother, of course). But she didn't like it—said it was hideous—so I gave her a bottle of scent instead. Now, of course, it's worth a packet. You can get Sowerby's to auction it, and the proceeds would certainly pay for the publication of the poems, if necessary. But only in the last resort, mind you! I'm convinced those poems can stand on their own. I'm only sorry I didn't finish the volcano one—maybe I could dictate it—'

'I really must get some sleep,' I broke in, thinking what a good thing it was they hadn't got STD yet between this world and the next. 'I'll go round to your flat first thing tomorrow. I've still got the key. Goodbye, Patrick.'

And I clonked back the receiver on its rest and tried to return to my lovely deep-hidden jampot factory among the brooding Downs. Gone beyond recall.

Next day at Patrick's flat I found I had been forestalled. The caretaker told me that a lady, Mrs O'Shea, had already called there and taken away all her son's effects.

I was wondering how to inform Patrick of this development—he hadn't left a number—when he got through to me again on his own phone. At the news I had to relate he let out a cry of anguish.

'Not Mother! God, what'll we do now? Ellis, that woman's a vulture. You'll have the devil's own job prising the poems out of her.'

'Why not just get in touch with her direct—the way you did with me—and tell *her* to send the poems to a publisher?' I said. 'Suggest trying Chatto first.'

'You don't understand! For one thing, I couldn't get near her. For another, she had this grudge against me; when I gave up going home it really dealt her a mortal blow. It'd give her the most exquisite pleasure to thwart me. No, I'm afraid you'll have to use all your tact and diplomacy, Ellis; you'd better drive down to Clayhole tomorrow—'

'But look here! Supposing she won't—'

No answer. Patrick had disconnected.

So next afternoon found me driving down to Clayhole. I had never been to Patrick's home—nor had Patrick, since the quarrel with his mother. I was quite curious to see her, as a matter of fact; Patrick's descriptions of her had been so conflicting. Before the breach she was the most wonderful mother in the world, fun, pretty, sympathetic, witty—while after it, no language had been too virulent to describe her, a sort of female Dracula, tyrannical, humourless, bloodsucking.

One thing I did notice as I approached the house—up a steep, stony, unmetalled lane—the weather had turned a bit colder. The leaves hung on the trees like torn rags, the ground was hard as iron, the sky leaden.

Mrs O'Shea received me with the utmost graciousness. But in spite of this I retained a powerful impression that I had arrived at an awkward moment; perhaps she had been about to bath the dog, or watch a favourite programme, or start preparing a meal. She was a small, pretty Irishwoman, her curling hair a beautiful white, her skin a lovely tea-rose pink, her eyes the curious opaque blue that goes with real granite obstinacy. One odd feature of her face was that she appeared to have no lips; they were so pale they disappeared into her powdered cheeks. I could see why Patrick had never mentioned his father. Major O'Shea stood beside his wife, but he was a nonentity; a stooped, watery-eyed, dangling fellow, whose only function was to echo his wife's opinions.

The house was a pleasant Queen Anne manor, furnished in excellent taste with chintz and Chippendale, and achingly, freezingly cold. I had to clench my teeth to stop them chattering. Mrs O'Shea in her cashmere twinset and pearls, seemed impervious to the glacial temperature, but the Major's cheeks were blue; every now and then a drop formed at the tip of his nose which he carefully wiped away with a spotless silk handkerchief. I began to understand why Patrick had been keen on volcanoes.

They stood facing me like an interview board while I explained my errand. I began by saying how grieved I had been to hear of Patrick's death, and spoke of his lovable nature and unusual promise. The Major did look genuinely grieved, but Mrs O'Shea was smiling, and there was something about her smile that irritated me profoundly.

I then went on to say that I had received a communication from Patrick since his death, and waited for reactions. They were sparse. Mrs O'Shea's lips tightened fractionally, the Major's lids dropped over his lugubrious milky-tea-coloured eyes; that was all.

'You don't seem surprised,' I said cautiously. 'You were expecting something of the kind perhaps?'

'No, not particularly,' Mrs O'Shea said. She sat down, placed her feet on a footstool and picked up a circular embroidery frame. 'My family is psychic, however; this kind of thing is not unusual. What did Patrick want to say?'

'It was about his poems.'

'Oh yes?' Her tone was as colourless as surgical spirit. She carefully chose a length of silk. Her glanced flickered once to the object she was using as a footstool: a solid pile of papers about a foot thick, wrapped up clumsily in an old grey cardigan which looked as if it had once lined a dog-basket; it was matted with white terrier-hairs.

My heart sank.

'I believe you have his poems now? Patrick is most anxious that they should be published.'

'And I'm not at all anxious they should be published,' Mrs O'Shea said with her most irritating smile.

'Quite, quite,' the Major assented.

We argued about it. Mrs O'Shea had three lines of argument: first, that no one in her family had ever written poetry, therefore Patrick's poems were sure to be hopeless; second, that no one in her family had ever written poetry and, even in the totally unlikely event of the poems being any good, it was a most disreputable thing to do; third, that Patrick was conceited, ungrateful, and self-centred, and it would do him nothing but harm to see his poems in print. She spoke as if he were still alive.

'Besides,' she added, 'I'm sure no publisher would look at them.'

'You have read them?'

'Heavens, no!' she laughed. 'I've no time for such rubbish.'

'But if a publisher did take them?'

'You'd never get one to risk his money on such a venture.'

I explained Patrick's plans regarding the Chapdelaine portrait. The O'Sheas looked sceptical. 'You perhaps have it here?' I asked.

'A hideous thing. Nobody in their senses would give enough money for that to get a book published.'

'I'd very much like to see it, all the same.'

'Roderick, take Miss Bell to look at the picture,' Mrs O'Shea said, withdrawing another strand of silk.

The picture was in the attic, face down. I saw at once why Mrs O'Shea had not liked it. Chapdelaine had done a merciless job of work. It was brilliant—one of the best examples of his early Gold Period. I imagined it would fetch even more than Patrick hoped. When I explained this to the Major an acquisitive gleam came into his eye.

'Surely that would more than pay for the publication of the poems?'

'Oh, certainly,' I assured him.

'I'll see what my wife has to say.'

Mrs O'Shea was not interested in cash. She had a new line of defence. 'Of course you've no actual proof that you come from Patrick, have you? I don't really see why we should take your word in the matter.'

Suddenly I was furious. My rage and the deadly cold were simultaneously too much for me. I said, as politely as I could, 'Since I can see you are completely opposed to my performing this small service for your son I won't waste any more of our time,' and then left abruptly. The Major looked a little taken aback, but his wife calmly pursued her stitchery.

It was good to get out of that icy, lavender-scented morgue into the fresh, windy night.

My car limped down the lane pulling to the left but I was so angry that I had reached the village before I realized I had a flat tyre. I got out and surveyed it. The car was slumped down on one haunch as if Mrs O'Shea had put a curse on it.

I went into the pub for a hot toddy before changing the wheel and while I was in there the landlord said, 'Would you be Miss

Bell? There's a phone call for you.'

It was Patrick. I told him about my failure and he cursed, but he did not seem surprised.

'Why does your mother hate you so, Patrick?'

'Because I got away from her. That's why she can't stand my poetry—because it's nothing to do with her. Anyway she can hardly read. If my father so much as picks up a book she gets it away from him as soon as she can and hides it. Well, you can see what he's like. Sucked dry. She likes to feel she knows the whole contents of a person's mind, and that it's entirely focused on *her*. She's afraid of being left alone; she's never slept by herself in a room in her life. If ever he had to go away she'd have my bed put in her room.'

I thought about that.

'But as to your authority to act for me,' Patrick went on. 'We can easily fix that. Have a double whisky and get a pen and paper. Shut your eyes.'

Reluctantly I complied. It was an odd sensation. I felt Patrick's light, chill clutch on my wrist, moving my hand. For a moment, the contrast with the last time I had held his hand made a strangling weight of tears in my throat; then I remembered Mrs O'Shea's icy determination, and realized that Patrick resembled her in this; suddenly I felt free of him, free of sorrow.

When I opened my eyes again, there was a message in Patrick's odd, angular script, to the effect that he authorized me to sell his Chapdelaine picture and use the proceeds to pay for the publication of his poems, if necessary.

The drinks had fortified me, so I got a garage to change my wheel and walked back up the lane to Clayhole. The O'Sheas had just finished their supper. They invited me civilly, but without enthusiasm, to drink coffee with them. The coffee was surprisingly good, but stone-cold, served in little gold-rimmed cups the size of walnut shells. Over it Mrs O'Shea scanned Patrick's message. I glanced round—we were in the arctic dining-room—and noticed that Chapdelaine's picture had now been hung on the wall. It smiled at me with Mrs O'Shea's own bland hostility.

'I see; very well,' she said at last. 'I suppose you must take the picture then.'

'And the poems, too, I hope.'

'Oh no. Not yet,' she said. '*When* you've sold the picture, for this large sum you say it will fetch, *then* I'll see about letting you have the poems.'

'But that's not—' I began, and then stopped. What was the use?

She was not a logical woman, no good reasoning with her. One step at a time was as fast as one could go.

The sale of an early Chapdelaine portrait made quite a stir, and the bidding at Sowerby's began briskly. The picture was exhibited on an easel on the auctioneer's dais. From my seat in the front row I was dismayed to notice, as the bids rose past the four-figure mark, that the portrait was beginning to fade. The background remained, but by the time twenty-five hundred had been reached, Mrs O'Shea had vanished completely. The bidding faltered and came to a stop; there were complaints. The auctioneer inspected the portrait, directed an accusing stare at me, and declared the sale null. I had to take the canvas ignominiously back to my flat, and the evening papers had humourous headlines: *Where did the colours run to? No bids for Chapdelaine's White Period.*

When the telephone rang I expected that it would be Patrick and picked up the receiver gloomily, but it was a French voice.

'Armand Chapdelaine here. Miss Bell?'

'Speaking.'

'We met, I think, once, a few years ago, in the company of young Patrick O'Shea. I am ringing from Paris about this odd incident of his mother's portrait.'

'Oh yes?'

'May I come and inspect the canvas, Miss Bell?'

'Of course,' I said, slightly startled. 'Not that there's anything to see.'

'That is so kind of you. Till tomorrow, then.'

Chapdelaine was a French Canadian: stocky, dark, and full of *loup-garou* charm.

After carefully scrutinizing the canvas he listened with intense interest to the tale about Patrick and his mother.

'Aha! This is a genuine piece of necromancy,' he said, rubbing his hands. 'I always knew there was something unusually powerful about that woman's character. She had a most profound dislike for me; I recall it well.'

'Because you were her son's friend.'

'Of course.' He inspected the canvas again and said, 'I shall be delighted to buy this from you for two thousand five hundred pounds, Miss Bell. It is the only one of my pictures that has been subjected to black magic, up to now.'

'Are you quite sure?'

'Entirely sure.' He gave me his engagingly wolfish smile. 'Then we will see what shot Madame Mère fetches out of her locker.'

Mrs O'Shea was plainly enjoying the combat over Patrick's poems. It had given her a new interest. When she heard the news that two thousand five hundred pounds was lodged in a trust account, ready to pay for the publication of the poems if necessary, her reaction was almost predictable.

'But that wouldn't be honest!' she said. 'I suppose Mr Chapdelaine bought the canvas out of kindness, but it can't be counted as a proper sale. The money must be returned to him.' Her face set like epoxy and she rearranged her feet more firmly on the footstool.

'On no account will I have it back, madame,' Chapdelaine riposted. He had come down with me to help her persuade her; he said he was dying to see her again.

'If you won't then it must be given to charity. I'm afraid it's out of the question that I should allow money which was obtained by what amounts to false pretences to be used to promote that poor silly boy's scribblings.'

'Quite, quite,' said the Major.

'But it may not be necessary—' I began in exasperation. An opaque blue gleam showed for an instant in Mrs O'Shea's eye. Chapdelaine raised a hand soothingly and I subsided. I'd known, of course, that I too was an object of her dislike, but I had not realized how very deep it went; the absolute hatred in her glance was a slight shock. It struck me that, unreasonably enough, this hate had been augmented by the fact that Chapdelaine and I were getting on rather well together.

'Since Madame does not approve of our plan I have another proposition,' said Chapdelaine, who seemed to be taking a pleasure in the duel almost equal to that of Mrs O'Shea. I felt slightly excluded. 'May I be allowed to do a second portrait, and two thousand five hundred shall be the sitter's fee?'

'Humph,' said Mrs O'Shea. 'I'd no great opinion of the last one ye did.'

'Hideous thing. Hideous,' said the Major.

'Oh, but this one, madame, will be quite different!' Chapdelaine smiled, at his most persuasive. 'In the course of seven years, after all, one's technique alters entirely.'

She demurred for a long time but in the end, I suppose, she could not resist this chance of further entertainment. Besides he was extremely well known now.

'You'll have to come down here, though, Mr Chapdelaine; at

my age I can't be gadding up to London for sittings.'

'Of course,' he agreed, shivering slightly; the sitting-room was as cold as ever. 'It will be a great pleasure.'

'I think the pub in the village occasionally puts up visitors,' Mrs O'Shea added. 'I'll speak to them.' Chapdelaine shuddered again. 'But they only have one bedroom, so I'm afraid there won't be room for *you*, Miss Bell.' Her tone expressed volumes.

'Thank you but I have my job in London,' I said coldly. 'Besides I'd like to be getting on with offering Patrick's poems; may I take them now, Mrs O'Shea?'

'The?—Oh, gracious, *no*—not till the picture's finished! After all,' she said, with a smile of pure, chill malice, 'I may not like it when it's done, may I?'

'It's a hopeless affair, hopeless!' I raged, as soon as we were away from the house. 'She'll always find some way of slipping out of the bargain; she's utterly unscrupulous. The woman's a fiend! Really I can't think how Patrick could have been fond of her. Why do you bother to go on with this?'

'Oh, but I am looking forward to painting this portrait immensely!' Chapdelaine wore a broad grin. 'I feel convinced this will be the best piece of work I ever did. I shall have to get that house warmed up, though, even if it means myself paying for a truckload of logs; one cannot work inside of a deep-freeze.'

Somehow he achieved this; when I took down a photographer to get a story, with pictures, for the magazine on which I work, we found the sitting-room transformed, littered with artists' equipment and heated to conservatory temperature by a huge roaring fire. Mrs O'Shea, evidently making the most of such unaccustomed sybaritude, was seated close by the fire, her feet, as ever, firmly planted on the blanket-wrapped bundle. She seemed in high spirits. The Major was nowhere to be seen; he had apparently been banished to some distant part of the house. Chapdelaine, I thought, did not look well; he coughed from time to time, complained of damp sheets at the pub, and constantly piled more logs on the fire. We took several shots of them both, but Mrs O'Shea would not allow us to see the uncompleted portrait.

'Not till it's quite done!' she said firmly. Meanwhile it stood on its easel in the corner, covered with a sheet, like some hesitant ghost.

During this time I had had numerous calls from Patrick, of course; he was wildly impatient about the slow progress of the painting.

'Do persuade Armand to go a bit faster, can't you, Ellis? He used to be able to dash off a portrait in about four sittings.'

'Well, I'll pass on your message, Patrick, but people's methods change, you know.'

When I rang Clayhole next day, however, I was unable to get through; the line was out of order, apparently, and remained so; when I reported this to the local exchange the girl said, 'Double four six three . . . wait a minute; yes, I thought so. We had a nine-nine-nine call from them not long ago. Fire brigade. No, that's all I can tell you, I'm afraid.'

With my heart in my suède boots I got out the car and drove down to Clayhole. The lane was blocked by police trucks, fire engines, and appliances; I had to leave my car at the bottom and walk up.

Clayhole was a smoking ruin; as I arrived they were just carrying the third blackened body out to the ambulance.

'What began it?' I asked the fire chief.

'That'll be for the insurance assessors to decide, miss. But it's plain it started in the lounge; spark from the fire, most likely. Wood fires are always a bit risky, in my opinion. You get that green apple wood—'

A spark, of course; I thought of the jersey-wrapped pile of poems hardly a foot distant from the crackling logs.

'You didn't find any papers in that room?'

'Not a scrap, miss; that being where the fire started, everything was reduced to powder.'

When Patrick got through to me that evening he was pretty distraught.

'She planned the whole thing!' he said furiously. 'I bet you, Ellis, she had it all thought out from the start. There's absolutely nothing that woman won't do to get her own way. Haven't I always said she was utterly unscrupulous? But I shan't be beaten by her, I'm just as determined as she is—*Do* pay attention Ellis!'

'Sorry, Patrick. What were you saying?' I was very low-spirited, and his next announcement did nothing to cheer me.

'I'll dictate you the poems, it shouldn't take more than a month or so if we keep at it. We can start right away. Have you a pen? And you'll want quite a lot of paper. I've finished the volcano poem, so we may as well start with that—ready?'

'I suppose so.' I shut my eyes. The cold clutch on my wrist was like a fetter. But I felt that, having gone so far, I owed this last service to Patrick.

'Right—here we go.' There followed a long pause. Then he said, with a good deal less certainty:

On each hand the flames
Driven backward slope their pointing spires—

'That's from *Paradise Lost*, Patrick,' I told him gently.

'I know . . .' His voice was petulant. 'That isn't what I meant to say. The thing is—it's starting to get so cold here. Oh, God, Ellis—it's so *cold* . . .'

His voice petered out and died. The grasp on my wrist became freezing, became numbing, and then, like a melted icicle, was gone.

'Patrick?' I said. 'Are you there, Patrick?'

But there was no reply, and indeed, I hardly expected one. Patrick never got through to me again. His mother had caught up with him at last.

Dylan Thomas

The Tree

Rising from the house that faced the Jarvis hills in the long distance, there was a tower for the day-birds to build in and for the owls to fly around at night. From the village the light in the tower window shone like a glow-worm through the panes; but the room under the sparrows' nests was rarely lit; webs were spun over its unwashed ceilings; it stared over twenty miles of the up-and-down county, and the corners kept their secrets where there were claw marks in the dust.

The child knew the house from roof to cellar; he knew the irregular lawns and the gardener's shed where flowers burst out of their jars; but he could not find the key that opened the door of the tower.

The house changed to his moods, and a lawn was the sea or the shore or the sky or whatever he wished it. When a lawn was a sad mile of water, and he was sailing on a broken flower down the waves, the gardener would come out of his shed near the island of bushes. He too would take a stalk, and sail. Straddling a garden broom, he would fly wherever the child wished. He knew every story from the beginning of the world.

'In the beginning,' he would say, 'there was a tree.'

'What kind of a tree?'

'The tree where that blackbird's whistling.'

'A hawk, a hawk,' cried the child.

The gardener would look up at the tree, seeing a monstrous hawk perched on a bough or an eagle swinging in the wind.

The gardener loved the Bible. When the sun sank and the garden was full of people, he would sit with a candle in his shed, reading of the first love and the legend of apples and serpents. But the death of Christ on a tree he loved most. Trees made a fence around him, and he knew of the changing of the seasons by the hues on the bark and the rushing of sap through the covered roots. His world moved and changed as spring moved along the branches, changing their nakedness; his God grew up like a tree from the apple-shaped earth, giving bud to His children and letting His children be blown from their places by the breezes of winter; winter and death moved in one wind. He would sit in his shed and read of the crucifixion, looking over the jars on his window-shelf into the winter nights. He would think that love fails on such nights, and that many of its children are cut down.

The child transfigured the blowsy lawns with his playing. The gardener called him by his mother's name, and seated him on his knee, and talked to him of the wonders of Jerusalem and the birth in the manger.

'In the beginning was the village of Bethlehem,' he whispered to the child before the bell rang for tea out of the growing darkness.

'Where is Bethlehem?'

'Far away,' said the gardener, 'in the East.'

To the east stood the Jarvis hills, hiding the sun, their trees drawing up the moon out of the grass.

The child lay in bed. He watched the rocking-horse and wished that it would grow wings so that he could mount it and ride into the Arabian sky. But the winds of Wales blew at the curtains, and crickets made a noise in the untidy plot under the window. His toys were dead. He started to cry and then stopped, knowing no reason for tears. The night was windy and cold, he was warm under the sheets; the night was as big as a hill, he was a boy in bed.

Closing his eyes, he stared into a spinning cavern deeper than the darkness of the garden where the first tree on which the unreal birds had fastened stood alone and bright as fire. The tears ran back under his lids as he thought of the first tree that was planted so near him, like a friend in the garden. He crept out of bed and tiptoed to the door. The rocking-horse bounded forward on its springs, startling the child into a noiseless scamper back to bed. The child looked at the horse and the horse was quiet; he tiptoed again along the carpet, and reached the door, and turned the knob around, and ran on to the landing. Feeling blindly in front of him, he made his way to the top of the stairs; he looked down the dark stairs into the hall, seeing a host of shadows curve in and out of the corners, hearing their sinuous voices, imagining the pits of their eyes and their lean arms. But they would be little and secret and bloodless, not cased in invisible armour but wound around with cloths as thin as a web; they would whisper as he walked, touch him on the shoulder, and say S in his ear. He went down the stairs; not a shadow moved in the hall, the corners were empty. He put out his hand and patted the darkness, thinking to feel some dry and velvet head creep under the fingers and edge, like a mist, into the nails. But there was nothing. He opened the front door, and the shadows swept into the garden.

Once on the path, his fears left him. The moon had lain down on the unweeded beds, and her frosts were spread on the grass. At last he came to the illuminated tree at the long gravel end, older even than the marvel of light, with the woodlice asleep under the bark, with the boughs standing out from the body like the frozen arms of a woman. The child touched the tree; it bent as to his touch. He saw a star, brighter than any in the sky, burn steadily above the first birds' tower, and shine on nowhere but on the leafless boughs and the trunk and the travelling roots.

The child had not doubted the tree. He said his prayers to it, with knees bent on the blackened twigs the night wind fetched to the ground. Then, trembling with love and cold, he ran back over the lawns towards the house.

There was an idiot to the east of the county who walked the land like a beggar. Now at a farmhouse and now at a widow's cottage he begged for his bread. A parson gave him a suit, and it lopped round his hungry ribs and shoulders and waved in the wind as he shambled over the fields. But his eyes were so wide and his neck so clear of the country dirt that no one refused him what he asked. And asking for water, he was given milk.

'Where do you come from?'

'From the east,' he said.

So they knew he was an idiot, and gave him a meal to clean the yards.

As he bent with a rake over the dung and the trodden grain, he heard a voice rise in his heart. He put his hand into the cattle's hay, caught a mouse, rubbed his hand over its muzzle, and let it go away.

All day the thought of the tree was with the child; all night it stood up in his dreams as the star stood above its plot. One morning towards the middle of December, when the wind from the farthest hills was rushing around the house, and the snow of the dark hours had not dissolved from lawns and roofs, he ran to the gardener's shed. The gardener was repairing a rake he had found broken. Without a word, the child sat on a seedbox at his feet, and watched him tie the teeth, and knew that the wire would not keep them together. He looked at the gardener's boots, wet with snow, at the patched knees of his trousers, at the undone buttons of his coat, and the folds of his belly under the patched flannel shirt. He looked at his hands as they busied themselves over the golden knots of wire; they were hard, brown hands, with the stains of the soil under the broken nails and the stains of tobacco on the tips of the fingers. Now the lines of the gardener's face were set in determination as time upon time he knotted the iron teeth only to feel them shake insecurely from the handle. The child was frightened of the strength and uncleanliness of the old man; but, looking at the long, thick beard, unstained and white as fleece, he soon became reassured. The beard was the beard of an apostle.

'I prayed to the tree,' said the child.

'Always pray to a tree,' said the gardener, thinking of Calvary and Eden.

'I pray to the tree every night.'

'Pray to a tree.'

The wire slid over the teeth.

'I pray to that tree.'

The wire snapped.

The child was pointing over the glasshouse flowers to the tree that, alone of all the trees in the garden, had no sign of snow.

'An elder,' said the gardener, but the child stood up from his box and shouted so loud that the unmended rake fell with a clatter on the floor.

'The first tree. The first tree you told me of. In the beginning was the tree, you said. I heard you,' the child shouted.

'The elder is as good as another,' said the gardener, lowering his voice to humour the child.

'The first tree of all,' said the child in a whisper.

Reassured again by the gardener's voice, he smiled through the window at the tree, and again the wire crept over the broken rake.

'God grows in strange trees,' said the old man. 'His trees come to rest in strange places.'

As he unfolded the story of the twelve stages of the cross, the tree waved its boughs to the child. An apostle's voice rose out of the tarred lungs.

So they hoisted him up on a tree, and drove nails through his belly and his feet.

There was the blood of the noon sun on the trunk of the elder, staining the bark.

*   *   *

The idiot stood on the Jarvis hills, looking down into the immaculate valley from whose waters and grasses the mists of morning rose and were lost. He saw the dew dissolving, the cattle staring into the stream, and the dark clouds flying away at the rumour of the sun. The sun turned at the edges of the thin and watery sky like a sweet in a glass of water. He was hungry for light as the first and almost invisible rain fell on his lips; he plucked at the grass, and, tasting it, felt it lie green on his tongue. So there was light in his mouth, and light was a sound at his ears, and the whole dominion of light in the valley that had such a curious name. He had known of the Jarvis hills; their shapes rose over the slopes of the county to be seen for miles around, but no one had told him of the valley lying under the hills. Bethlehem, said the idiot to the valley, turning over the sounds of the word and giving it all the glory of the Welsh morning. He brothered the world around him, sipped at the air, as a child newly born sips and brothers the light. The life of the Jarvis valley, steaming up from the body of the grass and the trees and the long hand of the stream, lent him a new blood. Night had emptied the idiot's veins, and dawn in the valley filled them again.

'Bethlehem,' said the idiot to the valley.

The gardener had no present to give the child, so he took out a key from his pocket and said: 'This is the key to the tower. On Christmas Eve I will unlock the door for you.'

Before it was dark, he and the child climbed the stairs to the tower, the key turned in the lock, and the door, like the lid of a secret box, opened and let them in. The room was empty. 'Where are the secrets?' asked the child, staring up at the matted rafters and into the spider's corners and along the leaden panes of the window.

'It is enough that I have given you the key,' said the gardener, who believed the key of the universe to be hidden in his pocket along with the feathers of birds and the seeds of flowers.

The child began to cry because there were no secrets. Over and over again he explored the empty room, kicking up the dust to look for a colourless trap-door, tapping the unpanelled walls for the hollow voice of a room beyond the tower. He brushed the webs from the window, and looked out through the dust into the snowing Christmas Eve. A world of hills stretched far away into the measured sky, and the tops of the hills he had never seen climbed up to meet the falling flakes. Woods and rocks, wide seas of barren land, and a new tide of mountain sky sweeping through the black beeches, lay before him. To the east were the outlines of nameless hill creatures and a den of trees.

'Who are they? Who are they?'

'They are the Jarvis hills,' said the gardener, 'which have been from the beginning.'

He took the child by the hand and led him away from the window. The key turned in the lock.

That night the child slept well; there was power in snow and darkness; there was unalterable music in the silence of the stars; there was a silence in the hurrying wind. And Bethlehem had been nearer than he expected.

*　　*　　*

On Christmas morning the idiot walked into the garden. His hair was wet and his flaked and ragged shoes were thick with the dirt of the fields. Tired with the long journey from the Jarvis hills, and weak for the want of food, he sat down under the elder-tree where the gardener had rolled a log. Clasping his hands in front of him, he saw the desolation of the flower-beds and the weeds that grew in profusion on the edges of the paths. The tower stood up like a tree of stone and glass over the red eaves. He pulled his coat-collar round his neck as a fresh wind sprang up and struck the tree; he looked down at his hands and saw that they were praying. Then a fear of the garden came over him, the shrubs were his enemies, and the trees that made an avenue down to the gate lifted their arms in horror. The place was too high, peering down on to the tall hills; the place was too low, shivering up at the plumed shoulders of a new mountain. Here the wind was too wild, fuming about the silence, raising a Jewish voice out of the elder boughs; here the silence beat like a human heart. And as he sat under the cruel hills, he heard a voice that was in him cry out: 'Why did you bring me here?'

He could not tell why he had come; they had told him to come and had guided him, but he did not know who they were. The voice of a people rose out of the garden beds, and rain swooped down from heaven.

'Let me be,' said the idiot, and made a little gesture against the sky. There is rain on my face, there is wind on my cheeks. He brothered the rain.

So the child found him under the shelter of the tree, bearing the torture of the weather with a divine patience, letting his long hair blow where it would, with his mouth set in a sad smile.

Who was this stranger? He had fires in his eyes, the flesh of his neck under the gathered coat was bare. Yet he smiled as he sat in his rags under a tree on Christmas Day.

'Where do you come from?' asked the child.

'From the east,' answered the idiot.

The gardener had not lied, and the secret of the tower was true; this dark and shabby tree, that glistened only in the night, was the first tree of all.

But he asked again:

'Where do you come from?'

'From the Jarvis hills.'

'Stand up against the tree.'

The idiot, still smiling, stood up with his back to the elder.

'Put out your arms like this.'

The idiot put out his arms.

The child ran as fast as he could to the gardener's shed, and, returning over the sodden lawns, saw that the idiot had not moved but stood, straight and smiling, with his back to the tree and his arms stretched out.

'Let me tie your hands.'

The idiot felt the wire that had not mended the rake close round his wrists. It cut into the flesh, and the blood from the cuts fell shining on to the tree.

'Brother,' he said. He saw that the child held silver nails in the palm of his hand.

Angus Wilson

Necessity's Child

Four years ago I still could know the seashore, especially the summer seashore of purple sea anemones, of ribbon weed clear like coal tar soap, of plimsoll rubber slipping upon seaweed slime, of crab bubbles from beneath the rock ledge—but now I have grown up—thirteen years old, too old to make my bucket the Sargasso Sea, too old to play at weddings in the cliff cave, too old to walk with handkerchief falling round my calf from a knee cut afresh each day on the rocks. Now there is only the great, far-stretching sea that frightens me. If I were like other boys, I should be getting to know the sea by swimming in it, treating it as my servant, somewhere to show off my strength, to dart in and out of the waves like a salmon, to lie basking on the surface like a seal. Mummy and Daddy and Uncle Reg can move like that. At one time they tried to teach me to join them, but now they have given me up as hopeless. I can watch their movements and wish to imitate them, but when I am in the water I am afraid. I am so alone there, its great strength is too great, it draws me under. I can lie on the beach and dream—I am Captain Scott watching the sea leopard catch the awkward penguins; I am the White Seal as he swam past the great, browsing sea cows; I am Salar the Salmon as he sported in the weir; I am Tarka the Otter as he learned to swim downstream; above all nowadays I am lying in the sun on the deck of the *Pequod* with the Southern Cross above me. But there always comes the moment of fear—Captain Scott has dread in his heart as he reaches the Pole too late; the dart from the jaws of the conger eel; Tarka lies taut beneath the river bank as the hounds breathe overhead; on the *Pequod* is heard the ominous tapping of Ahab's ivory leg. Even in my dream I must be afraid, must feel unprotected.

Mummy and Daddy are ashamed of my fears. They play games that are meant to be for my benefit, but they are their games really. I spoilt cricket on the beach as I used to spoil their sandcastles. When we were playing last summer, Mummy called out that she did not want me on her side. 'I'm not having Rodney on our side,' she said, 'I want to win.' 'We'll have to have you on *our* side, old man,' Daddy said, 'if your mother doesn't want you. I think we can carry a rabbit, don't you, Reggie?' and Uncle Reggie said, 'Yes, you'll have to be the tail, Rodney. With luck it'll be lunch-time before the last man goes in.' It was just the same building sandcastles when I was little. Once I started to make a ruined tower. 'What on earth is that, darling?' Mummy asked me, and when I told her, 'Ruined is about right,' she said. 'Derek, my dear, what can make him suppose that we want a ruined tower when we're building the Clifton suspension bridge?' 'Ye olde ruined and medieval suspension bridge, eh Rodney?' said Uncle Reggie. But Daddy just took the sand to build one of his pediments. In the end I used to fetch and carry for them. 'Get us some sea-water in that bucket, there's a good little chap,' or, 'Darling, just dig all round here for me.' Sometimes I used to forget about the game and stand dreaming, then it used to be, 'Don't stand on the drawbridge, old chap, that'll never do,' or, 'Darling, if Uncle Reggie takes the trouble to make this marvellous fort for you, I *do* think you might take some interest.'

The truth is that I am a bit in the way. I heard Mummy telling Auntie Eileen about it one afternoon in the garden. 'Well there it is,' she said, 'we can never have another and so we must face the situation. But you can say what you like, Eileen, I'm not having a mother's darling around the place. I suppose it's very awful of me to say so, but I realize now that the whole thing was the greatest mistake. Derek and I aren't the sort of people to make parents. We married because we were in love, we still are and we're going to stay that way. We like having fun and we like having it together. Derek doesn't want to come home to someone who's old and tired and scratchy at the end of the day and I intend to see that he doesn't.' Auntie Eileen thinks she can make up for it, she's kind to me and when I was little it was nice to play with her. But Mummy's right when she says that she's silly. She doesn't under-stand anything. She just likes to share silly secrets. 'Well, Rodney, what little stories have you been making up today?' She likes to show off when people are there, too. She winks at me with her stupid fat sheep's face. 'Rodney and I have lots of little secrets, haven't we?' She made me ashamed when she came down to the Christmas play, talking to Mr Rogers like that. 'I'm not a bit surprised at Rodney's acting so well. You see we've always been rather special friends and we've had our little plays since he was ever so small.' But she didn't notice the look on Mr Roger's face.

I wish I was back at school. I wish this holiday was over. There'll be nets and missing catches, I know, and the bridge ladder and not knowing the answers in algebra and old Puffin banging his ruler down so that you can't think. 'If you can't deal with X and Y, try and think what the answer would be if it was pears and apples, or the beloved pineapple chunks,' as if *that* made it any easier. But then there'll be Tony and Gerald to talk to. Gerald said that he would read *Moby Dick* too, when Mr Rogers told us about it, and even if Tony can't manage it, and lots of it *is* difficult to understand, we can tell him about all the important bits like Ahab's fight with the white whale, and the sea-hawk, and Quee-queg praying to his idol. We'll all have read *The Wreckers*, too, because Mr Rogers set it as holiday reading, we'll be able to act lots of it and with any luck they'll let me act Pinkerton. Mr Rogers said we should read *Barnaby Rudge* for English, it will be the last book I shall read in class at St Bertram's, because in the autumn I shall be going on to Uppingham. To a public school! Mummy and Daddy like to talk about it, but I try not to listen because I'm so frightened. Oh God don't let me think about it! Oh God don't let me think about it! If I count one hundred and three before I get to the kiosk I shan't ever go to a public school. One, two, three, four, five, six, seven, eight . . .

'Talking to yourself? That's bad, that's very bad': the thick, unctuous voice sounded stern, but jolly. Rodney, startled out of his thoughts, stared up at the flabby and rubicund face of Mr Cartwright, the vicar of St Barnabas'. 'You know what they say about people who talk to themselves, don't you? Just a little bit cracked, getting ready for the loony bin,' and Mr Cartwright laughed with schoolboy glee. 'I'm afraid I didn't know I was doing it,' mumbled Rodney. 'That's no excuse in the eyes of the law,' boomed Mr Cartwright, all mock magisterial severity. 'And how have the holidays been? Pretty busy, eh? Gordon and Roger have got a craze,' and he dwelt lovingly on what he felt to be the juvenile *mot juste*, 'on hockey at the moment. They tell me you don't play. You know, I'll let you into a secret if you won't tell the boys,' he looked all conspiratorial, 'I've no use for the game either. Fast enough, I know, but it always seems to me something of a girl's game. I tell you what though, Mr Harker's lent the boys the gym at the High School, you must come up one evening for a rag.'

Rodney murmured an assent, then, as Mr Cartwright continued to talk of his sons and the April Fool they had played upon him, he suddenly became panic-stricken at the thought of the commitment. I can't go up there, I won't.

'I'm afraid I shan't be able to come after all,' he interrupted Mr Cartwright breathlessly. 'You see Mummy's ill and she likes me to be about to help in the house.'

'Oh! I'm sorry to hear that,' said the vicar. 'Not seriously I hope. Mrs Cartwright will want to call and help when she hears.'

'Oh, please, no visitors or telephones at the moment,' said Rodney.

'Dear, oh, dear. *You* must keep us posted then. It's a fine thing for you that you can be such a help at this time. A great fellow like you can do a lot to earn your living. You'll be leaving St Bertram's soon for a wider world, I suppose. Uppingham, isn't it? That's something to look forward to. Though mind you,' and his voice took on a confirmation-class note, 'it won't be all beer and skittles at first. One gets to be rather a big pot at one's prep school, and unfortunately when one goes on to a public school they don't seem to quite see things that way. But you'll soon settle down. It's just a question,' he added with ringing confidence, 'of not getting rattled.'

He's speaking about it as though it was certain to happen, as though it didn't matter, thought Rodney. How can I make myself not mind going there, if there are people like him about who take all the bullying for granted, who seem to want it. If none of it can happen to me, I won't even let *him* think it can. Aloud he said 'I know heaps of other boys there already, so I expect I shall be all right.'

'Good show,' said Mr Cartwright. 'Well, we shall expect to hear great things of you,' and with a pat on the boy's shoulder, he set off along the parade.

I've told him two lies, thought Rodney, and they're bound to be found out. It's always happening like that. Why didn't I say that I didn't want his rotten rag in the gym? Why did I have to say I knew people at Uppingham when I didn't? Because you were afraid of his knowing you were frightened. And now Mummy and Daddy will find out that I lied and they'll despise me for it. If I was dying like Thatcher when he had meningitis, they wouldn't want me always to be with other boys, they would want to have me with *them*. If Daddy was to die, I should be very brave and Mummy would be very proud of me. The schoolroom is filled for evening prayers when old Puffin calls out loudly, 'Brent, will you step outside please, we have some rather serious news about your father.' White-faced and tense, but steady, I walk out of the room. Mummy is sitting weeping in Puffin's study. 'I don't need an explanation, sir, I think I understand. My father is dead!' and then with my arms round her, 'Don't cry, darling, I will try to be all he would have wanted me to be,' and then to Puffin, 'I think, sir, if you could get my mother a little brandy.' Making up horrible daydreams, that's all I ever do. I can't be any good except in my imagination. It's not fair, really, there's nothing to be brave about, when all that is wanted of you is to keep out of the way. I shall sit in the shelter here and read *The Wreckers* until long after supper time and then perhaps they'll wonder where I am and get worried about me.

The problem of the mysterious cargo of the wrecked ship was so absorbing that it was some time before Rodney noticed that he had been joined in the shelter by two other people. The stout old lady in the heavy fur coat was the first to speak. 'You *must* have an interesting book to be carried away like that,' she said. Rodney decided that with her long face, her tiny eyes, and the warts on her cheek she looked like a huge furry hippopotamus. 'A really good yarn on a nice spring day. What could be jollier?' said the old gentleman in slow, mournful tones, which seemed somehow accentuated by the downward curve of his long white moustaches and the watery blue of his protruding pug's eyes.

'It's Robert Louis Stevenson's *Wreckers*,' said Rodney with some pride.

'Ah!' said the old gentleman, 'the redoubtable Pinkerton. Somebody you're not familiar with, my dear,' he added to his wife, 'not unlike that American we met last year who'd patented those revolting and peculiarly useless braces.'

'I don't think I should have particularly wanted to read about him,' said his wife. 'He had such very bad manners. But, there I expect it would be different if it was in a book.'

'My wife's one of those unfortunate people who can't read,' said the old gentleman with great seriousness. The old lady protested laughingly and an expression of puzzled concern appeared on Rodney's face. 'Well, it's almost true,' the old gentleman went on. 'She never learnt the delight of books until she was too old. Now when I was your age I lived half my time in the stories I read, as I've no doubt you do. I remembering being D'Artagnan for weeks on end—a great, swaggering Gascon fellow, I'm not sure it wasn't then that I grew these moustaches. One thing I am sure of, though, I didn't keep to the book exactly. I remember I always saved milady from the block at the last minute. I know, of course, that she wasn't exactly a nice person, but still it's always the mark of a cad to refuse to help a beautiful woman when she's in trouble.'

'I love the chapters where milady seduces Felton,' said Rodney.

'Ah! yes, a nice juicy bit,' said the old gentleman, looking sideways at his wife's shocked expression. 'There's no need for alarm, my dear, the word seduce is used only in a very general sense, to imply dereliction of duty and that sort of thing, you know. But my wife does like *one* book,' he turned to Rodney, 'our grandchildren read it to her last winter, and that's *Wind in the Willows*. Of course, she fell in love with Toad.'

'I didn't,' protested the old lady. 'I thought he was odious.' 'Oh! he wasn't really,' said Rodney. 'He was really a nice, kind sort of person, only he boasted rather a lot.'

'Yes, yes,' said the old gentleman. 'We're none of us free from weaknesses, not even you, my dear. And then he was a pioneer of motoring, though whether that's on the credit side I'm not so sure. However he had a proper sense of his superiority to the teaching profession, which our friend here no doubt shares. "The clever men at Oxford know all there is to be knowed",' he recited, laughing heartily.

' "But there's none of them knows half as much as intelligent Mr Toad",' finished Rodney and he began to laugh too.

His enjoyment was suddenly halted, however, by the lady's next remark.

'I expect you read lots of books aloud to *your* mother,' she said.

Rodney paused some moments before answering.

'Yes,' he said at last, 'you see Mummy's an invalid and she depends a lot on me.'

'I'm sure you're a great help to her,' said the old lady. 'What does your father do?'

'Daddy's a solicitor,' replied Rodney. 'Poor Daddy!' he added with a deep sigh.

'That's a very large sigh for so small a person,' said the old lady.

'I was just thinking how difficult it is when people don't understand each other. Daddy's such a kind man really, only he gets so angry because Mummy's always snapping. It's only because she has dreadful pain to bear, but Daddy doesn't seem to understand. That's what makes him drink so. When he gets drunk he says dreadful things to Mummy and then she wishes she could die.'

'Never mind, my dear,' said the old lady. 'If I understand how your Mummy feels, having you about will make life worth living.'

'That's what Daddy says,' Rodney went on in increasingly excited tones. 'We had wonderful walks together in the country and along the seashore. He knows all about birds and fishes and makes everything so interesting. If only Mummy knew what he was like then, oh! I wish I could make them understand each other. I think I'm the only person who could.'

The old gentleman left off drawing lines in the gravel with his walking stick. He looked quizzically for a moment at Rodney, then he said drily, 'Making human beings understand one another can be quite a difficult task.'

Rodney's look of bewilderment as he replied was appealing in its innocence. 'Oh! I know how difficult it will be, and after all I am only a child.'

The old gentleman's tone was more kindly, as rising from the seat he patted Rodney's shoulder. 'I shouldn't worry too much if I were you, grown-up people are very strange creatures,' he said. 'They often seem to be in a bad way, but it's amazing how quickly they pull out of it. Well, we must be going, my dear,' he added.

The old lady bent down and kissed Rodney's forehead, then she produced a visiting card from her handbag. 'If you're ever in need of a friend, this is my name and address,' she said. 'I shall always think of you as a very brave boy.'

It was well after tea when Rodney returned home, but Mrs Brent did not appear to notice that he was late. For a moment as he saw her he remembered his lies to the vicar and wondered with dread whether Mrs Cartwright had rung up. But his trained eye soon saw from his mother's face that no storm was brewing, and with long acquired habit he pushed his fears aside. It hasn't led to trouble yet, he thought: perhaps if I cross my fingers it never will. 'Please God, if it's all right this time I'll never tell any more stories,' he murmured.

Mummy was wearing her black costume with the diamond shoulder clip, he noticed, and the black hat with the cock-feathers that curled over the ear. That meant that Daddy and she must be going out. They had only been in to dinner four times during the holidays and then there had been visitors so that he had to have supper on his own. If only they would talk to him occasionally. Of course, Mummy *did* sometimes, but only if there was nobody there, and *usually* if they were alone, she would say, 'Thank goodness! an afternoon to ourselves. Now I can get on with something. I hope you've got things to do, Rodney, because I really must get this finished before Daddy comes home and I don't want to be constantly interrupted.' Anyhow Auntie Eileen was here for her to talk to this evening. Certainly no one could want a better listener, he thought, as he watched his aunt's pale moonface with its look of constant surprise, the eyebrows raised and the mouth eternally rounded and ready with exclamations of 'Oh!' or 'No!' to greet the speaker, her large ear-rings jangling with interest.

'Quite honestly, Eileen, I think she must have been canned,' his mother was saying. 'She's never a good player, but to go up five in a major suit, when she didn't even hold the top two honours, *and* they were vulnerable. Of course Derek was *furious*. I've promised him we'll never go there again. But it's a frightful bore, because she's been so useful over petrol coupons.'

'Oh! Vera, how maddening for you!' said her sister-in-law.

'Yes, it is rather, isn't it? Actually, of course, Derek's bridge is so much too good for this town, that it's rather a bore playing anyway. You should see the look on the poor lamb's face sometimes when one of these old girls makes some terrible call. Anyhow the summer's coming now so that with tennis and cricket there won't be much time for bridge. You know the new road-house has opened on the London Road?'

'No!' said Eileen. 'Really? I didn't know.'

It was amazing how few things his aunt *did* know Rodney reflected.

'Yes, my dear, and it's really awfully gay. We're motoring out there this evening after drinks at the Grahams'. Derek's crazy to take up dancing in a big way again. He adores all this old-time dancing. So the summer programme will be pretty full. There really *does* look to be a chance of our getting abroad at the end of August. Derek says all the money restrictions mean nothing if you know the ropes.'

'Rodney will like that,' said Aunt Eileen.

'My dear,' replied Mrs Brent, 'I honestly think it would be madness to take him. Nothing could be less amusing for a child than a Paris holiday, and it wouldn't be terribly fair on us. No, thank goodness! The house-master at Uppingham has been amazingly kind about it, he's quite willing for him to arrive there a few weeks early and be a sort of paying guest. There'll be other boys there, too, which will be very good for him.'

'Oh Mummy please!' Rodney cried, 'don't make me go there in the holidays. It'll be awful, I know it will.'

'My dear child, there's no need to get excited. We're not proposing to send you to prison or something. It'll be a marvellous chance to get to know some of the boys before term begins. You'll be one up on the other new boys.'

'Rodney can come to me, Vera, if he likes,' and Aunt Eileen wrinkled her nose intimately at her nephew. 'We'd have grand times.'

'There you are, Rodney. You can go to Auntie Eileen's though I'm not sure it wouldn't be better if you were to be with other boys.'

'I don't *want* to go to Auntie Eileen's,' Rodney almost shouted. 'I want to be with you and Daddy.'

'Well, I'm afraid you'll have to want. Daddy and I are going abroad. And now apologize to your aunt for being so rude.' It was no good putting everybody against you, thought Rodney, so he said 'I'm sorry, Auntie Eileen.' Then suddenly he kicked at the table. 'But everything's so jolly dull, I get so bored and that makes me cross.'

'What have you been doing this afternoon that bored your lordship so?' said his mother.

'Talking to an old lady and gentleman on the front.'

'Well really! Rodney. With hundreds of other children in the town you spend the afternoon talking to some old couple and then you say you're bored. I give up!'

'What about your book?' said Auntie Eileen. 'You're not the person to be dull if there's a book about.'

'Oh it's all right,' said Rodney, 'but I'm tired of reading.'

'Why not make up a story for yourself?' said Auntie Eileen. 'That ought to be great fun and then you can tell it to me.'

'Don't spoil the child,' said his mother and she began to tell her sister-in-law of their holiday plans.

Half an hour later Rodney's father returned. 'Hullo Eileen,' he said to his sister, 'What's the best news?' He leant over his wife's chair and kissed her, running his hands down her breasts. 'Had a good day, Tuppence?' he said. His wife's somewhat hard, carefully made-up face softened as she answered, 'This is the best moment.' 'Same here,' he replied, smiling boyishly. 'How's the world treating you, old son?' he called to Rodney. 'He's been an absolute horror,' said Mrs Brent. 'Bad show,' said her husband. 'We must be moving, darling.' 'You looked tired, sweet,' said Mrs Brent. 'I am a bit,' said her husband. 'Then *I* shall drive.' 'I won't say no,' and he gave her a smack on the bottom as he pushed her out of the room. 'Pass along the car there,' he called.

'Will you be all right, Rodney, while I get your supper?' said Auntie Eileen. 'Then we can have a nice long chat.' 'I'm busy making up a story like you told me,' said her nephew and he smiled to himself.

A quarter of an hour later when Auntie Eileen returned bringing a cup of Bovril and some jam tart on a tray, Rodney was sitting in the chair, his body tense and his face white and strained.

'Rodney, darling, what is the matter?' she cried. 'Oh! it's so horrible,' the boy said, his eyes rounded. 'I couldn't tell Mummy. I can't tell anyone ever.'

'You can tell *me*, darling.'

'Oh I do so want to. But if I do, you'll tell Mummy. Promise if I tell that you'll keep it a secret.'

'Of course, of course I promise,' said Auntie Eileen with relish.

'It happened this afternoon with that old gentleman,' said Rodney speaking in an excited, staccato voice. 'He looked so nice, Auntie, and then he showed me pictures, horrible, beastly pictures.'

'Oh! my darling,' said Auntie Eileen, 'how dreadful! What a wicked, wicked man!' Then she added, 'But I thought you said there was an old lady with him. Had she gone away or what?'

There was a short silence and then, 'No, Auntie,' said Rodney bitterly, 'No she was there. She just laughed and said they had lots more like that at home and I'd better come back and see them, but I ran away. Promise, promise you'll never tell anyone, it was all so dreadful I don't want to think about it ever again.'

'I wish I knew what was right,' said Auntie Eileen, but at Rodney's look of alarm she added, 'Very well, darling, it'll be our secret we'll just forget. But I shall always think of you as a very brave boy.'

The sea swings away from me now, brown and sandy in patches, but without light, grey and cold. It heaves and tosses and lashes itself into white fury, as it crashes and thunders against the breakwater. It flies into a mist that sprays against my cheeks. But always, however the waves may rush forward, tumbling over each other to smash upon the beach, the sea swings towards me and away from me. I am sitting upon a raft and the calm, level water is swinging me so, back and forward. It is the Pacific Ocean everywhere, clear and green. Over the side of the raft I can see deep, deep down to strange, coloured fishes and seahorses and coral. I am all alone, 'alone on a wide, wide sea'. Mummy and Daddy have gone down with the ship, spinning round and round like the *Pequod*, See! She sinks in a whirlpool and I am shot out, far out, alone on this raft. The heat will scorch and burn me, 'the bloody sun at noon', and thirst and the following sharks. Don't let me be alone so, don't let me think of that. But now the sea is moving, violently, wildly in high Atlantic waves. I am lashed to a raft, the sea is swinging me roughly, up on the crest so that the wing of the albatross or the seahawk brushes my cheek, raucous screams are in my ears, hooked beaks snap at my eyes, and now down, down into the trough where the white whale waits. Mummy and Daddy have gone down with the ship. It crashed and broke against the glass-green wall, the name *Titanic* staring forth in red letters as it reared into the air. Mummy's black evening dress floated on the surface of the water and her shoulder showed white as she was sucked down. But I am left alone, tied to the raft, numbed, frozen, choking with the cold, or again, as it sails relentlessly on towards the next floating green giant, dashing me to pieces against ice as I fight with the ropes too securely tied.

The Star Child

Once upon a time two poor Woodcutters were making their way home through a great pine-forest. It was winter, and a night of bitter cold. The snow lay thick upon the ground, and upon the branches of the trees: the frost kept snapping the little twigs on either side of them, as they passed: and when they came to the Mountain-Torrent she was hanging motionless in air, for the Ice-King had kissed her.

So cold was it that even the animals and the birds did not know what to make of it.

'Ugh!' snarled the Wolf, as he limped through the brushwood with his tail between his legs, 'this is perfectly monstrous weather. Why doesn't the Government look to it?'

'Weet! weet! weet!' twittered the green Linnets, 'the old Earth is dead, and they have laid her out in her white shroud.'

'The Earth is going to be married, and this is her bridal dress,' whispered the Turtle-doves to each other. Their little pink feet were quite frost-bitten, but they felt that it was their duty to take a romantic view of the situation.

'Nonsense!' growled the Wolf. 'I tell you that it is all the fault of the Government, and if you don't believe me I shall eat you.' The Wolf had a thoroughly practical mind, and was never at a loss for a good argument.

'Well, for my own part,' said the Woodpecker, who was a born philosopher, 'I don't care an atomic theory for explanations. If a thing is so, it is so, and at present it is terribly cold.'

Terribly cold it certainly was. The little Squirrels, who lived inside the tall fir-tree, kept rubbing each other's noses to keep themselves warm, and the Rabbits curled themselves up in their holes, and did not venture even to look out of doors. The only people who seemed to enjoy it were the great horned Owls. Their feathers were quite stiff with rime, but they did not mind, and they rolled their large yellow eyes, and called out to each other across the forest, 'Tu-whit! Tu-whoo! Tu-whit! Tu-whoo! What delightful weather we are having!'

On and on went the two Woodcutters, blowing lustily upon their fingers, and stamping with their huge iron-shod boots upon the caked snow. Once they sank into a deep drift, and came out as white as millers are, when the stones are grinding; and once they slipped on the hard smooth ice where the marsh-water was frozen, and their faggots fell out of their bundles, and they had to pick them up and bind them together again; and once they thought that they had lost their way, and a great terror seized on them, for they knew that the Snow is cruel to those who sleep in her arms. But they put their trust in the good Saint Martin, who watches over all travellers, and retraced their steps, and went warily, and at last they reached the outskirts of the forest, and saw, far down in the valley beneath them, the lights of the village in which they dwelt.

So overjoyed were they at their deliverance that they laughed aloud, and the Earth seemed to them like a flower of silver, and the Moon like a flower of gold.

Yet, after that they had laughed they became sad, for they remembered their poverty, and one of them said to the other, 'Why did we make merry, seeing that life is for the rich, and not for such as we are? Better that we had died of cold in the forest, or that some wild beast had fallen upon us and slain us.'

'Truly,' answered his companion, 'much is given to some, and little is given to others. Injustice has parcelled out the world, nor is there equal division of aught save of sorrow.'

But as they were bewailing their misery to each other this strange thing happened. There fell from heaven a very bright and beautiful star. It slipped down the side of the sky, passing by the other stars in its course, and, as they watched it wondering, it seemed to them to sink behind a clump of willow-trees that stood hard by a little sheepfold no more than a stone's-throw away.

'Why! there is a crock of gold for whoever finds it,' they cried, and they set to and ran, so eager were they for the gold.

And one of them ran faster than his mate, and outstripped him, and forced his way through the willows, and came out on the other side, and lo! there was indeed a thing of gold lying on the white snow. So he hastened towards it, and stooping down placed his hands upon it, and it was a cloak of golden tissue, curiously wrought with stars, and wrapped in many folds. And he cried out to his comrade that he had found the treasure that had fallen from the sky, and when his comrade had come up, they sat them down in the snow, and loosened the folds of the cloak that they might divide the pieces of gold. But, alas! no gold was in it, nor silver, nor, indeed, treasure of any kind, but only a child who was asleep.

And one of them said to the other: 'This is a bitter ending to our hope, nor have we any good fortune, for what doth a child profit to a man? Let us leave it here, and go our way, seeing that we are poor men, and have children of our own whose bread we may not give to another.'

But his companion answered him: 'Nay, but it were an evil thing to leave the child to perish here in the snow, and though I am as poor as thou art, and have many mouths to feed, and but little in the pot, yet will I bring it home with me, and my wife shall have care of it.'

So very tenderly he took up the child, and wrapped the cloak around it to shield it from the harsh cold, and made his way down the hill to the village, his comrade marvelling much at his foolishness and softness of heart.

And when they came to the village, his comrade said to him, 'Thou hast the child, therefore give me the cloak, for it is meet that we should share.'

But he answered him: 'Nay, for the cloak is neither mine nor thine, but the child's only,' and he bade him Godspeed, and went to his own house and knocked.

And when his wife opened the door and saw that her husband had returned safe to her, she put her arms round his neck and kissed him, and took from his back the bundle of faggots, and brushed the snow off his boots, and made him come in.

But he said to her, 'I have found something in the forest, and I have brought it to thee to have care of it,' and he stirred not from the threshold.

'What is it?' she cried. 'Show it to me, for the house is bare, and we have need of many things.' And he drew the cloak back, and showed her the sleeping child.

'Alack, goodman!' she murmured, 'have we not children enough of our own, that thou must needs bring a changeling to sit by the hearth? And who knows if it will not bring us bad fortune? And how shall we tend it?' And she was wroth against him.

'Nay, but it is a Star-Child,' he answered; and he told her the strange manner of the finding of it.

But she would not be appeased, but mocked at him, and spoke angrily, and cried: 'Our children lack bread, and shall we feed the child of another? Who is there who careth for us? And who giveth us food?'

'Nay, but God careth for the sparrows even, and feedeth them,' he answered.

'Do not the sparrows die of hunger in the winter?' she asked. 'And is it not winter now?' And the man answered nothing, but stirred not from the threshold.

And a bitter wind from the forest came in through the open door, and made her tremble, and she shivered, and said to him: 'Wilt thou not close the door? There cometh a bitter wind into the house, and I am cold.'

'Into a house where a heart is hard cometh there not always a bitter wind?' he asked. And the woman answered him nothing, but crept closer to the fire.

And after a time she turned round and looked at him, and her eyes were full of tears. And he came in swiftly, and placed the child in her arms, and she kissed it, and laid it in a little bed where the youngest of their own children was lying. And on the morrow the Woodcutter took the curious cloak of gold and placed it in a great chest, and a chain of amber that was round the child's neck his wife took and set it in the chest also.

So the Star-Child was brought up with the children of the Woodcutter, and sat at the same board with them, and was their playmate. And every year he became more beautiful to look at, so that all those who dwelt in the village were filled with wonder, for, while they were swarthy and black-haired, he was white and delicate as sawn ivory, and his curls were like the rings of the daffodil. His lips, also, were like the petals of a red flower, and his eyes were like violets by a river of pure water, and his body like the narcissus of a field where the mower comes not.

Yet did his beauty work him evil. For he grew proud, and cruel, and selfish. The children of the Woodcutter, and the other children of the village, he despised, saying that they were of mean parentage, while he was noble, being sprung from a Star, and he made himself master over them, and called them his servants. No pity had he for the poor, or for those who were blind or maimed or in any way afflicted, but would cast stones at them and drive them forth on to the highway, and bid them beg their bread elsewhere, so that none save the outlaws came twice to that village to ask for alms. Indeed, he was as one enamoured of beauty, and would mock at the weakly and ill-favoured, and make jest of them; and himself he loved, and in summer, when the winds were still, he would lie by the well in the priest's orchard and look down at the marvel of his own face, and laugh for the pleasure he had in his fairness.

Often did the Woodcutter and his wife chide him, and say: 'We did not deal with thee as thou dealest with those who are left desolate, and have none to succour them. Wherefore art thou so cruel to all who need pity?'

Often did the old priest send for him, and seek to teach him the love of living things, saying to him: 'The fly is thy brother. Do it no harm. The wild birds that roam through the forest have their freedom. Snare them not for thy pleasure. God made the blind-worm and the mole, and each has its place. Who art thou to bring pain into God's world? Even the cattle of the field praise him.'

But the Star-Child heeded not their words, but would frown and flout, and go back to his companions, and lead them. And his companions followed him, for he was fair, and fleet of foot, and could dance and pipe, and make music. And wherever the Star-Child led them they followed, and whatever the Star-Child bade them do, that did they. And when he pierced with a sharp reed the dim eyes of the mole, they laughed, and when he cast stones at the leper they laughed also. And in all things he ruled them, and they became hard of heart even as he was.

Now there passed one day through the village a poor beggar-woman. Her garments were torn and ragged, and her feet were bleeding from the rough road on which she had travelled, and she was in very evil plight. And being weary she sat her down under a chestnut-tree to rest.

But when the Star-Child saw her, he said to his companions, 'See! There sitteth a foul beggar-woman under that fair and green-leaved tree. Come, let us drive her hence, for she is ugly and ill-favoured.'

So he came near and threw stones at her, and mocked her, and she looked at him with terror in her eyes, nor did she move her gaze from him. And when the Woodcutter, who was cleaving logs in a haggard hard by, saw what the Star-Child was doing, he ran up and rebuked him, and said to him: 'Surely thou art hard of heart and knowest not mercy, for what evil has this poor woman done to thee that thou shouldst treat her in this wise?'

And the Star-Child grew red with anger, and stamped his foot upon the ground, and said, 'Who art thou to question me what I do? I am no son of thine to do thy bidding.'

'Thou speakest truly,' answered the Woodcutter, 'yet did I

show thee pity when I found thee in the forest.'

And when the woman heard these words she gave a loud cry and fell into a swoon. And the Woodcutter carried her to his own house, and his wife had care of her, and when she rose up from the swoon into which she had fallen, they set meat and drink before her, and bade her have comfort.

But she would neither eat nor drink, but said to the Woodcutter, 'Didst thou not say that the child was found in the forest? And was it not ten years from this day?'

And the Woodcutter answered, 'Yea, it was in the forest that I found him, and it is ten years from this day.'

'And what signs didst thou find with him?' she cried. 'Bare he not upon his neck a chain of amber? Was not round him a cloak of gold tissue broidered with stars?'

'Truly,' answered the Woodcutter, 'it was even as thou sayest.' And he took the cloak and the amber chain from the chest where they lay, and showed them to her.

And when she saw them she wept for joy, and said, 'He is my little son whom I lost in the forest. I pray thee send for him quickly, for in search of him have I wandered over the whole world.'

So the Woodcutter and his wife went out and called to the Star-Child, and said to him, 'Go into the house, and there shalt thou find thy mother, who is waiting for thee.'

So he ran in, filled with wonder and great gladness. But when he saw her who was waiting there, he laughed scornfully and said, 'Why, where is my mother? For I see none here but this vile beggar-woman.'

And the woman answered him, 'I am thy mother.'

'Thou art mad to say so,' cried the Star-Child angrily. 'I am no son of thine, for thou art a beggar, and ugly, and in rags. Therefore get thee hence, and let me see thy foul face no more.'

'Nay, but thou art indeed my little son, whom I bare in the forest,' she cried, and she fell on her knees, and held out her arms to him. 'The robbers stole thee from me, and left thee to die,' she murmured, 'but I recognized thee when I saw thee, and the signs also have I recognized, the cloak of golden tissue and the amber chain. Therefore I pray thee come with me, for over the whole world have I wandered in search of thee. Come with me, my son, for I have need of thy love.'

But the Star-Child stirred not from his place, but shut the doors of his heart against her, nor was there any sound heard save the sound of the woman weeping for pain.

And at last he spoke to her, and his voice was hard and bitter. 'If in very truth thou art my mother,' he said, 'it had been better hadst thou stayed away, and not come here to bring me to shame, seeing that I thought I was the child of some Star, and not a beggar's child, as thou tellest me that I am. Therefore get thee hence, and let me see thee no more.'

'Alas! my son,' she cried, 'wilt thou not kiss me before I go? For I have suffered much to find thee.'

'Nay,' said the Star-Child, 'but thou art too foul to look at, and rather would I kiss the adder or the toad than thee.'

So the woman rose up, and went away into the forest weeping bitterly, and when the Star-Child saw that she had gone, he was glad, and ran back to his playmates that he might play with them.

But when they beheld him coming, they mocked him and said, 'Why, thou art as foul as the toad, and as loathsome as the adder. Get thee hence, for we will not suffer thee to play with us,' and they drave him out of the garden.

And the Star-Child frowned and said to himself, 'What is this that they say to me? I will go to the well of water and look into it, and it shall tell me of my beauty.'

So he went to the well of water and looked into it, and lo! his face was as the face of a toad, and his body was scaled like an adder. And he flung himself down on the grass and wept, and said to himself, 'Surely this has come upon me by reason of my sin. For I have denied my mother, and driven her away, and been proud, and cruel to her. Wherefore I will go and seek her through the whole world, nor will I rest till I have found her.'

And there came to him the little daughter of the Woodcutter, and she put her hand upon his shoulder and said, 'What doth it matter if thou has lost thy comeliness? Stay with us, and I will not mock at thee.'

And he said to her, 'Nay, but I have been cruel to my mother, and as a punishment has this evil been sent to me. Wherefore I must go hence, and wander through the world till I find her, and she give me forgiveness.'

So he ran away into the forest and called out to his mother to come to him, but there was no answer. All day long he called to her, and when the sun set he lay down to sleep on a bed of leaves, and the birds and the animals fled from him, for they remembered his cruelty, and he was alone save for the toad that watched him, and the slow adder that crawled past.

And in the morning he rose up, and plucked some bitter berries from the trees and ate them, and took his way through the great wood, weeping sorely. And of everything that he met he made inquiry if perchance they had seen his mother.

He said to the Mole, 'Thou canst go beneath the earth. Tell me, is my mother there?'

And the Mole answered, 'Thou hast blinded mine eyes. How should I know?'

He said to the Linnet, 'Thou canst fly over the tops of the tall trees, and canst see the whole world. Tell me, canst thou see my mother?'

And the Linnet answered, 'Thou hast clipt my wings for thy pleasure. How should I fly?'

And to the little Squirrel who lived in the fir-tree, and was lonely, he said, 'Where is my mother?'

And the Squirrel answered, 'Thou hast slain mine. Dost thou seek to slay thine also?'

And the Star-Child wept and bowed his head, and prayed forgiveness of God's things, and went on through the forest, seeking for the beggar-woman. And on the third day he came to the other side of the forest and went down into the plain.

And when he passed through the villages the children mocked him, and threw stones at him, and the carlots would not suffer him even to sleep in the byres lest he might bring mildew on the stored corn, so foul was he to look at, and their hired men drave him away, and there was none who had pity on him. Nor could he hear anywhere of the beggar-woman who was his mother, though for the space of three years he wandered over the world, and often seemed to see her on the road in front of him, and would call to her, and run after her till the sharp flints made his feet to bleed. But overtake her he could not, and those who dwelt by the way did ever deny that they had seen her, or any like to her, and they made sport of his sorrow.

For the space of three years he wandered over the world, and in the world there was neither love nor loving-kindness nor charity for him, but it was even such a world as he had made for himself in the days of his great pride.

And one evening he came to the gate of a strong-walled city that stood by a river, and weary and footsore though he was, he made to enter in. But the soldiers who stood on guard dropped their halberts across the entrance, and said roughly to him, 'What is thy business in the city?'

'I am seeking for my mother,' he answered, 'and I pray ye to suffer me to pass, for it may be that she is in this city.'

But they mocked at him, and one of them wagged a black beard, and set down his shield and cried, 'Of a truth, thy mother will not be merry when she sees thee, for thou art more ill-favoured than the toad of the marsh, or the adder that crawls in the fen. Get thee gone. Get thee gone. Thy mother dwells not in this city.'

And another, who held a yellow banner in his hand, said to him, 'Who is thy mother, and wherefore art thou seeking for her?'

And he answered, 'My mother is a beggar even as I am, and I have treated her evilly, and I pray ye to suffer me to pass that she may give me her forgiveness, if it be that she tarrieth in this city.' But they would not, and pricked him with their spears.

And, as he turned away weeping, one whose armour was inlaid with gilt flowers, and on whose helmet couched a lion that had wings, came up and made inquiry of the soldiers who it was who had sought entrance. And they said to him, 'It is a beggar and the child of a beggar, and we have driven him away.'

'Nay,' he cried, laughing, 'but we will sell the foul thing for a slave, and his price shall be the price of a bowl of sweet wine.'

And an old and evil-visaged man who was passing by called out, and said, 'I will buy him for that price,' and, when he had paid the price, he took the Star-Child by the hand and led him into the city.

And after that they had gone through many streets they came to a little door that was set in a wall that was covered with a pomegranate tree. And the old man touched the door with a ring of graved jasper and it opened, and they went down five steps of brass into a garden filled with black poppies and green jars of burnt clay. And the old man took then from his turban a scarf of figured silk, and bound with it the eyes of the Star-Child, and drave him in front of him. And when the scarf was taken off his eyes, the Star-Child found himself in a dungeon, that was lit by a lantern of horn.

And the old man set before him some mouldy bread on a trencher and said, 'Eat,' and some brackish water in a cup and said, 'Drink,' and when he had eaten and drunk, the old man went out, locking the door behind him and fastening it with an iron chain.

And on the morrow the old man, who was indeed the subtlest of the magicians of Libya and had learned his art from one who dwelt in the tombs of the Nile, came in to him and frowned at him, and said, 'In a wood that is nigh to the gate of this city of Giaours there are three pieces of gold. One is of white gold, and another is of yellow gold, and the gold of the third one is red. To-day thou shalt bring me the piece of white gold, and if thou bringest it not back, I will beat thee with a hundred stripes. Get thee away quickly, and at sunset I will be waiting for thee at the door of the garden. See that thou bringest the white gold, or it shall go ill with thee, for thou art my slave, and I have bought thee for the price of a bowl of sweet wine.' And he bound the eyes of the Star-Child with the scarf of figured silk, and led him through the house, and through the garden of poppies, and up the five steps of brass. And having opened the little door with his ring he set him in the street.

And the Star-Child went out of the gate of the city, and came to the wood of which the Magician had spoken to him.

Now this wood was very fair to look at from without, and seemed full of singing birds and of sweet-scented flowers, and the Star-Child entered it gladly. Yet did its beauty profit him little, for wherever he went harsh briars and thorns shot up from the ground and encompassed him, and evil nettles stung him and the thistle pierced him with her daggers, so that he was in sore distress. Nor could he anywhere find the piece of white gold of which the Magician had spoken, though he sought for it from morn to noon, and from noon to sunset. And at sunset he set his face towards home, weeping bitterly, for he knew what fate was in store for him.

But when he had reached the outskirts of the wood, he heard from a thicket a cry as of some one in pain. And forgetting his own sorrow he ran back to the place, and saw there was a little Hare caught in a trap that some hunter had set for it.

And the Star-Child had pity on it, and released it, and said to it, 'I am myself but a slave, yet may I give thee thy freedom.'

And the Hare answered him, and said: 'Surely thou has given me freedom, and what shall I give thee in return?'

And the Star-Child said to it, 'I am seeking for a piece of white gold, nor can I anywhere find it, and if I bring it not to my master he will beat me.'

'Come thou with me,' said the Hare, and I will lead thee to it, for I know where it is hidden, and for what purpose.'

So the Star-Child went with the Hare, and lo! in the cleft of a great oak-tree he saw the piece of white gold that he was seeking. And he was filled with joy, and seized it, and said to the Hare, 'The service that I did to thee thou hast rendered back again many times over, and the kindness that I showed thee thou has repaid a hundred-fold.'

'Nay,' answered the Hare, 'but as thou dealt with me, so I did deal with thee,' and it ran away swiftly, and the Star-Child went towards the city.

Now at the gate of the city there was seated one who was a leper. Over his face hung a cowl of grey linen, and through the eyelets his eyes gleamed like red coals. And when he saw the Star-Child coming, he struck upon a wooden bowl, and clattered his bell, and called out to him, and said, 'Give me a piece of money, or I must die of hunger. For they have thrust me out of the city, and there is no one who has pity on me.'

'Alas!' cried the Star-Child, 'I have but one piece of money in my wallet, and if I bring it not to my master he will beat me, for I am his slave.'

But the leper entreated him, and prayed of him, till the Star-Child had pity, and gave him the piece of white gold.

And when he came to the Magician's house, the Magician opened to him, and brought him in, and said to him, 'Hast thou the piece of white gold?' And the Star-Child answered, 'I have it not.' So the Magician fell upon him, and beat him, and set before him an empty trencher, and said, 'Eat,' and an empty cup, and said, 'Drink,' and flung him again into the dungeon.

And on the morrow the Magician came to him, and said, 'If to-day thou bringest me not the piece of yellow gold, I will surely keep thee as my slave, and give thee three hundred stripes.'

So the Star-Child went to the wood, and all day long he searched for the piece of yellow gold, but nowhere could he find it. And at sunset he sat him down and began to weep, and as he was weeping there came to him the little Hare that he had rescued from the trap.

And the Hare said to him, 'Why art thou weeping? And what dost thou seek in the wood?'

And the Star-Child answered, 'I am seeking for a piece of yellow gold that is hidden here, and if I find it not my master will beat me, and keep me as a slave.'

'Follow me,' cried the Hare, and it ran through the wood till it came to a pool of water. And at the bottom of the pool the piece of yellow gold was lying.

'How shall I thank thee?' said the Star-Child, 'for lo! this is the second time that you have succoured me.'

'Nay, but thou hadst pity on me first,' said the Hare, and it ran away swiftly.

And the Star-Child took the piece of yellow gold, and put it in his wallet, and hurried to the city. But the leper saw him coming, and ran to meet him, and knelt down and cried, 'Give me a piece of money or I shall die of hunger.'

And the Star-Child said to him, 'I have in my wallet but one piece of yellow gold, and if I bring it not to my master he will beat me and keep me as his slave.'

But the leper entreated him sore, so that the Star-Child had pity on him, and gave him the piece of yellow gold.

And when he came to the Magician's house, the Magician opened to him, and brought him in, and said to him, 'Hast thou the piece of yellow gold?' And the Star-Child said to him, 'I have not.' So the Magician fell upon him, and beat him, and loaded him with chains, and cast him again into the dungeon.

And on the morrow the Magician came to him, and said, 'If to-day thou bringest me the piece of red gold I will set thee free, but if thou bringest it not I will surely slay thee.'

So the Star-Child went to the wood, and all day long he searched for the piece of red gold, but nowhere could he find it. And at evening he sat him down and wept, and as he was weeping there came to him the little Hare.

And the Hare said to him, 'The piece of red gold that thou seekest is in the cavern that is behind thee. Therefore weep no more but be glad.'

'How shall I reward thee?' cried the Star-Child, 'for lo! this is the third time thou hast succoured me.'

'Nay, but thou hadst pity on me first,' said the Hare, and it ran away swiftly.

And the Star-Child entered the cavern, and in its farthest corner he found the piece of red gold. So he put it in his wallet, and hurried to the city. And the leper seeing him coming, stood in the centre of the road, and cried out, and said to him, 'Give me the piece of red money, or I must die,' and the Star-Child had pity on him again, and gave him the piece of red gold, saying. 'Thy need is greater than mine.' Yet his heart was heavy, for he knew what evil fate awaited him.

But lo! as he passed through the gate of the city, the guards bowed down and made obeisance to him, saying, 'How beautiful is our lord!' and a crowd of citizens followed him, and cried out, 'Surely there is none so beautiful in the whole world!' so that the Star-Child wept, and said to himself, 'They are mocking me, and making light of my misery.' And so large was the concourse of the people, that he lost the threads of his way, and found himself at last in a great square, in which there was a palace of a King.

And the gate of the palace opened, and the priests and the high officers of the city ran forth to meet him and they abased themselves before him, and said, 'Thou art our lord for whom we have been waiting, and the son of our King.'

And the Star-Child answered them and said, 'I am no king's son, but the child of a poor beggar-woman. And how say ye that I am beautiful, for I know that I am evil to look at?'

Then he, whose armour was inlaid with gilt flowers, and on whose helmet crouched a lion that had wings, held up a shield, and cried, 'How saith my lord that he is not beautiful?'

And the Star-Child looked, and lo! his face was even as it had been, and his comeliness had come back to him, and he saw that in his eyes which he had not seen there before.

And the priests and the high officers knelt down and said to him, 'It was prophesied of old that on this day should come he who was to rule over us. Therefore, let our lord take this crown and this sceptre, and be in his justice and mercy our King over us.'

But he said to them, 'I am not worthy, for I have denied the mother who bare me, nor may I rest till I have found her, and known her forgiveness. Therefore, let me go, for I must wander again over the world, and may not tarry here, though ye bring me the crown and the sceptre.' And as he spake he turned his face from them towards the street that led to the gate of the city, and lo! amongst the crowd that pressed round the soldiers, he saw the beggar-woman who was his mother, and at her side stood the leper, who had sat by the road.

And a cry of joy broke from his lips, and he ran over, and kneeling down he kissed the wounds on his mother's feet, and wet them with his tears. He bowed his head in the dust, and sobbing, as one whose heart might break, he said to her: 'Mother, I denied thee in the hour of my pride. Accept me in the hour of my humility. Mother, I gave thee hatred. Do thou give me love. Mother, I rejected thee. Receive thy child now.' But the beggar-woman answered him not a word.

And he reached out his hands, and clasped the white feet of the leper, and said to him: 'Thrice did I give thee of my mercy. Bid my mother speak to me once.' But the leper answered him not a word.

And he sobbed again and said: 'Mother, my suffering is greater than I can bear. Give me thy forgiveness, and let me go back to the forest.' And the beggar-woman put her hand on his head, and said to him, 'Rise,' and the leper put his hand on his head, and said to him, 'Rise,' also.

And he rose from his feet, and looked at them, and lo! they were a King and a Queen.

And the Queen said to him, 'This is thy father whom thou hast succoured.'

And the King said, 'This is thy mother whose feet thou hast washed with thy tears.'

And they fell on his neck and kissed him, and brought him into the palace and clothed him in fair raiment, and set the crown upon his head, and the sceptre in his hand, and over the city that stood by the river he ruled, and was its lord. Much justice and mercy did he show to all, and the evil Magician he banished, and to the Woodcutter and his wife he sent many rich gifts, and to their children he gave high honour. Nor would he suffer any to be cruel to bird or beast, but taught love and loving-kindness and charity, and to the poor he gave bread, and to the naked he gave raiment, and there was peace and plenty in the land.

Yet ruled he not long, so great had been his suffering, and so bitter the fire of his testing, for after the space of three years he died. And he who came after him ruled evilly.

Keith Waterhouse

Albert and the Liner

Below the military striking clock in the City Arcade there was, and for all I know still is, a fabulous toyshop.

It was a magic grotto, that shop. A zoo, a circus, a pantomime, a travelling show, a railway exhibition, an enchanted public library, a clockwork museum, an archive of boxed games, a pavilion of sports equipment, a depository of all the joys of the indefinite, endless leisure of the winter holiday — but first, the military striking clock.

Once a year we were taken to see the clock strike noon — an event in our lives as colourful, and traditional, and as fixed and immovable in the calendar of pageantry as Trooping the Colour. Everybody who was anybody assembled, a few minutes before twelve, on the patch of worn tiles incorporating an advertisement for tomato sausages done in tasteful mosaic, beneath that military striking clock.

There was me, and Jack Corrigan, and the crippled lad from No 43, and there was even Albert Skinner — whose father never took him anywhere, not even to the Education Office to explain why he'd been playing truant.

Albert Skinner, with his shaved head and his shirt-lap hanging out of his trousers, somehow attached himself, insinuated himself, like a stray dog. You'd be waiting at the tram stop with your mother, all dolled up in your Sunday clothes for going into town and witnessing the ceremony of the military striking clock, and Albert, suddenly, out of nowhere, would be among those present.

'Nah, then, kid.'

And your mother, out of curiosity, would say — as she was meant to say — 'You're never going into town looking like that are you, Albert?'

And Albert would say: 'No. I was, only I've lost my tram fare.'

And your mother, out of pity, would say — as she was meant to say — 'Well, you can come with us. But you'll have to tidy yourself up. Tuck your shirt in, Albert.'

So at Christmas time Albert tagged on to see the military

striking clock strike noon. And after the mechanical soldiers of the King had trundled back into their plaster-of-Paris garrison, he, with the rest of us, was allowed to press his nose to the fabulous toyshop window.

Following a suitable period of meditation, we were then treated to a bag of mint imperials — *'and think on, they're to share between you'* — and conveyed home on the rattling tram. And there, thawing out our mottled legs by the fireside, we were supposed to compose our petitions to Father Christmas.

Dear Father Christmas, for Christmas I would like . . .

'Don't know what to put,' we'd say at length to one another, seeking some kind of corporate inspiration.

'Why don't you ask him for a sledge? I am.'

'Barmpot, what do you want a sledge for? What if it doesn't snow?'

'Well — a cricket bat and stumps, and that.'

'Don't play cricket at Christmas, barmpot.'

Albert Skinner said nothing. Nobody, in fact, said anything worth saying, during those tortured hours of voluntary composition.

With our blank jumpo jotters on our knees, we would suck our copying-ink pencils until our tongues turned purple — but it wasn't that we were short of ideas. Far from it: sledges, cricket bats and stumps and that, fountain pens, dynamos, cinematographs complete with Mickey Mouse films — the fact of the matter was, there was too much choice.

For the fabulous toyshop, which sparked off our exotic and finally blank imaginations, was the nearest thing on this earth to Santa's Workshop. It was like a bankruptcy sale in heaven. The big clockwork train ran clockwise and the small electric train ran anti-clockwise, and there was Noah's Ark, and a tram conductor's set, and a junior typewriter revolving on a brightly-lit glass shelf, and a fairy cycle hanging from the ceiling on invisible wires, and a tin steam roller, and the Tip-Top Annual and the Film Fun Annual and the Radio Fun Annual and the Jingles Annual and the Joker Annual and the Jester Annual, and board games, and chemistry sets, and conjuring sets, and carpentry sets — everything, in short, that the modern boy would give his eye-teeth for.

Everything that Albert Skinner would have given his eye-teeth for, in fact, and much that Albert Skinner would never get. And not only him. There were items that no reasonable modern boy expected to find in his Christmas pillow-case — not even though he bartered every tooth in his head and promised to be a good lad till kingdom come.

The centrepiece of the fabulous toyshop's window display was always something out of the reach of ordinary mortals, such as the Blackpool Tower in Meccano, or a mechanical carousel with horses that went up and down on their brass poles like the real thing, or Windsor Castle made of a million building bricks, or Buckingham Palace with nobs on — floodlit. None of us had to be told that such luxuries were beyond Father Christmas's price range.

This year the window featured a splendid model of the *Queen Mary*, which had recently been launched on Clydebank. It was about four feet long, with real lights in the portholes, real steam curling out of the funnels, and a crew, and passengers, and lifeboats, and cabin trunks, all to scale — and clearly it was not for the likes of us.

Having seen it and marvelled at it, we dismissed this expensive dream from our minds, sucked our copying-ink pencils and settled down to list our prosaic requests — for Plasticine, for farmyard animals that poisoned you when you licked the paint off, and for one pair of roller skates between two of us.

All of us, that is to say, except Albert Skinner. Having considered several possibilities, and taken advice on the rival merits of a racing track with eight electric sports cars and a glove puppet of Felix the Cat he's rather fancied, Albert calmly announced that he'd given thought to all our suggestions and he was asking Father Christmas for the *Queen Mary*.

This, as you might imagine, was greeted with some scepticism.

'What — that one in the Arcade window? With all the lights and the steam coming out and that? You've never asked for that, have you?'

'Yeh — course I have. Why shouldn't I?'

'He's blinking crackers. Hey, Skinno, why don't you ask for them soldiers that march in and out and bang that clock? Because you've more chance of getting them than that *Queen Mary*.'

'If I'd wanted them soldiers I'd have asked for them. Only I don't. So I've asked him for the *Queen Mary*.'

'Who — Father Christmas?'

'No — him on the Quaker Oats Box, who do you think?'

'Bet you haven't, man. Bet you're having us on.'

'I'm not — God's honour. I've asked him for the *Queen Mary*.'

'Let's see the letter, then.'

'Can't — I've chucked it up the chimney.'

'Yeh — bet you have. Anyway, your dad won't get if for you — he can't afford it.'

'What's it got to do with him? I'm asking Father Stinking Rotten Christmas for it, not me dad. Dozy.'

'What else have you asked for, Skinno?'

'Nowt. I don't want owt else. I just want the *Queen Mary*. And I'm getting it, as well.'

Little else was said at the time, but privately we thought Albert was a bit of an optimist. For one thing, the *Queen Mary* was so big and so grand and so lit-up that it was probably not even for sale. For another, we were all well aware that Father Christmas's representative in the Skinner household was a sullen, foul-tempered collier who also happened to be unemployed.

Albert's birthday present, it was generally known, had been a pair of boots — instead of the scooter on which, at that time, he had set his heart.

Even so, Albert continued to insist that he was getting the *Queen Mary* for Christmas. 'Ask my dad,' he would say. 'If you don't believe me, ask my dad.'

None of us cared to broach to subject with the excitable Mr Skinner. But sometimes, when we went to his house to swop comics, Albert would raise the matter himself.

'Dad, I am aren't I? Aren't I, Dad? Getting that *Queen Mary* for Christmas?'

Mr Skinner, dourly whittling a piece of wood by the fireside after the habit of all the local miners, would growl without looking up: 'You'll get a cloud over the bloody earhole if you don't stop chelping.'

Albert would turn complacently to us. 'I am, see. I'm getting the *Queen Mary*. Aren't I, Dad? Dad? Aren't I?'

Sometimes, when his father had come home from the pub in a bad mood (which was quite often), Albert's pleas for reassurance would be met with a more vicious response. 'Will you shut up about the bloody Queen swining Mary!' Mr Skinner would shout. 'You gormless little git, do you think I'm made of money?'

Outside, his ear tingling from the blow his father had landed on it, Albert would bite back the tears and declare stubbornly: 'I'm still getting it. You wait till Christmas.'

Christmas Eve was but a fortnight off by then. Most of us had a shrewd idea, from hints dropped by our mothers, what Father Christmas would be bringing us — or, in most cases, not bringing.

'I don't think Father Christmas can manage an electric train set this year, our Terry. He says they're too expensive. He says he might be able to find you a tip-up lorry.'

Being realists, we accepted our lowly position on Father Christmas's scale of priorities — and we tried our best to persuade Albert to accept his.

'You're not *forced* to get that *Queen Mary*, you know, Skinno.'

'Who says I'm not?'

'My mam. She says it's too big to go in Father Christmas's sack.'

'Yeh, well that's all *she* knows. Because he's fetching Jacky Corrigan a fairy cycle — so if he can't get the *Queen Mary* in his sack, how can he get a stinking rotten fairy cycle?'

'Yeh, well he isn't fetching me a fairy cycle at all, clever-clogs, he's fetching me a John Bull printing outfit. 'Cos he told my mam.'

'I don't care what he told her, or what he didn't tell her. He's still fetching me that *Queen Mary*.'

The discussion was broken up by the sudden appearance of Mr Skinner at their scullery window. 'If I hear one more bloody word from you about that bloody *Queen Mary*, you'll get nothing for Christmas! Do you hear me?' And there the matter rested.

A few days later the crippled lad at No 43 was taken by the Church Ladies Guild to see the military striking clock in the City Arcade, and when he came home he reported that the model of the *Queen Mary* was no longer in the window of the fabulous toyshop.

'I know,' said Albert, having confirmed that his father was out of earshot. 'I'm getting it for Christmas.'

And indeed, it seemed the only explanation possible. The fabulous toyshop never changed its glittering display until after Boxing Day — it was unheard of. Some minor item might vanish out of the window — the Noah's Ark, perhaps, or a farmyard, or a game of Monopoly or two. There was a rational explanation for this: Father Christmas hadn't enough toys to go round and he'd been obliged, so to speak, to call on his sub-contractors. But the set-piece, the Blackpool Tower made out of Meccano or the carousel with the horses that went round and round and up and down — that was never removed; never. And yet the *Queen Mary* had gone. What had happened? Had Father Christmas gone mad? Had Mr Skinner bribed him — and if so, with what? Had Mr Skinner won the football pools? Or was it that Albert's unswerving faith could move mountains – not to mention ocean-going liners with real steam and real lights in the portholes? Or was it, as one cynic among us insisted, that the *Queen Mary* had been privately purchased for some pampered grammar school lad on the posher side of town?'

'You just wait and see,' said Albert.

And then it was Christmas morning; and after the chocolate pennies had been eaten and all the kitchens in the street were awash with nut-shells and orange peel, we all flocked out to show off our presents — sucking our brand-new torches to make our cheeks glow red, or brandishing a lead soldier or two in the pretence that we had a whole regiment of them indoors. Those who had wanted wooden forts were delighted with their painting books; those who had prayed for electric racing cars were content with their Dinky toys; those who had asked for roller skates were happy with their pencil boxes; and there was no sign of Albert.

No one, in fact, expected to see him at all. But just as we were asking each other what Father Christmas could have brought him — a new jersey, perhaps, or a balaclava helmet — he came bounding, leaping, jumping, almost somersaulting into the street. 'I've got it! I've got it! I've got it!'

Painting books and marbles and games of Happy Families were abandoned in the gutter as we clustered around Albert, who was cradling in his arms what seemed on first inspection to be a length of wood. Then we saw that it had been roughly carved at both ends, to make a bow and stern, and that three cotton-reels had been nailed to it for funnels. A row of tintacks marked the Plimsoll line, and there were stuck-on bits of cardboard for the portholes. The whole thing was painted over in sticky lamp-black, except for the lettering on the portside.

'*The Queen Mary*,' it said. In white, wobbling letters. Capital T, small he, capital E. Capital Q, small u, capital E, capital E, small n. Capital M, small a, capital R, small y. Penmanship had never been Mr Skinner's strong point.

'See!' crowed Albert complacently. 'I told you he'd fetch me it, and he's fetched me it.'

Our grunts of appreciation, though somewhat strained, were genuine enough. Albert's *Queen Mary* was a crude piece of work, but clearly many hours of labour, and much love, had gone into it. Its clumsy contours alone must have taken night after night of whittling by the fireside.

Mr Skinner, pyjama-jacket tucked into his trousers, had come out of the house and was standing by his garden gate. Albert, in a rush of happiness, ran to his father and flung his arms around him and hugged him. Then he waved the *Queen Mary* on high.

'Look, Dad! Look what I've got for Christmas! Look what Father Christmas has fetched me! You knew he would, didn't you, all this time!'

'Get out of it, you soft little bugger,' said Mr Skinner. He drew contentedly on his empty pipe, cuffed Albert over the head as a matter of habit, and went indoors.

Acknowledgements

The editor wishes to thank the authors (or their agents or trustees) and publishers who have granted permission to reproduce the following copyright material:

'Charles' by Shirley Jackson. Reprinted by permission of A.M. Heath & Co. Ltd.

'A Sound of Thunder' by Ray Bradbury. © 1952 by Ray Bradbury. © renewed 1980 by Ray Bradbury. Reprinted by permission of the Harold Matson Company Inc.

'The Edwin Tree' by Chris Hawes. Reprinted by permission of the author and Deborah Rogers Ltd.

'Grandpa' by James H. Schmitz. Reprinted by permission of the author and the author's agents, Scott Meredith Literary Agency Inc., 845 Third Avenue, New York, NY 10022.

'The Cold Flame' by Joan Aiken, from *A Bundle of Nerves* (Gollancz) and *the Fifth Ghost Book* (© 1969 by Barrie Books Ltd).

'The Tree' by Dylan Thomas, from *A Prospect of the Sea* (J.M. Dent). Reprinted by permission of David Higham Associates.

'Necessity's Child' by Angus Wilson, from *Such Darling Dodos* (Secker and Warburg Ltd).

'Albert and the Liner' by Keith Waterhouse, from *Dandelion Clocks* (Michael Joseph Ltd).